TOXIC LOVE

stories by
Linda Holeman

Tundra Books

Published in Canada by Tundra Books,
481 University Avenue, Toronto, Ontario M5G 2E9

Published in the United States by Tundra Books of Northern New
York, P.O. Box 1030, Plattsburgh, New York 12901

Original edition published in 1995 as *Saying Good-bye* by Lester
Publishing Limited.

Library of Congress Control Number: 2002114700

National Library of Canada Cataloguing in Publication

Holeman, Linda
    Toxic love / by Linda Holeman.

Originally publ. under title: Saying good-bye.
ISBN 0-88776-647-1

    I. Title. II. Title: Saying good-bye.

PS8565.O6225S29 2003   C813'.54   C2002-905307-2
PR9199.3.H5485S29 2003

We acknowledge the financial support of the Government of
Canada through the Book Publishing Industry Development
Program (BPIDP) and that of the Government of Ontario through
the Ontario Media Development Corporation's Ontario Book
Initiative. We further acknowledge the support of the Canada
Council for the Arts and the Ontario Arts Council for our
publishing program.

This is a work of fiction. Any resemblance to persons living or dead,
or to actual events, is purely coincidental.

Design: Cindy Reichle

Printed and bound in Canada

1 2 3 4 5 6   08 07 06 05 04 03

Contents

For my mother and father,
who shared their stories and listened to mine

Something Fishy

You know the fishwife, that old hag in the kids' story? She's always griping to her husband about how rotten her life is, about how she doesn't have what other fishermen's wives have. A real whiner.

One day Mr. Henpecked catches this magic fish, who says (I always figured the real magic was that he could talk) that the fisherman can have one wish. But instead of wishing for a new boat, or at least a new net, the guy goes home and tells his wife. Even though this is long before the women's movement, the wife figures the wish should be hers – and she nabs it, saying she wants to be a high-class lady. Voilà! There she is, all dressed up and living in a big house.

But soon she wants a bigger house and more clothes and jewels, so she sends Mr. Henpecked back out to sea again, to have a chat with the fish. Once again he snags it – what a coincidence – and he gets another wish. Or rather, his wife gets another wish.

The story goes on and on, with the wife eventually winding up as queen of all the land. But then she makes her big mistake. She wants to have it all, rule the earth and the sky *and* the sea. Bad judgment. The fish gets all bent out of shape and – *poof* – the woman is back to the hut on the beach, dressed in rags.

Seems as if what happened to that old lady, and to me, is what always happens when you get what you ask for.

You just want more.

I had a regular kind of life. So regular that it felt as though it belonged in a museum with all the other extinct things. It was like one of those old movies, where everyone was always polite and neat, and nothing serious ever went wrong. The kind of movie where the wife said things like "Happy, darling?" to her husband as they smiled at each other over the martinis they always had just before dinner.

Obviously ours is not your typical family. It's not separated, step, half, blended, or unique in any noticeable way. My father has a secure administrative job with the Wheat Board; he's been there since I was a baby and has no plans to leave until retirement. My mother was always "home" for us. In the last few years, however, it has dawned on her that she's on the verge of empty-nest syndrome, as well as closing in on menopause. This causes her to cry on a regular basis and use her NordicTrack with grim determination as she scans the classifieds, hoping to find the perfect part-time job to take her mind off her age.

I have an older brother, Richard, who's working toward a science degree at university. He never allows anyone to call him Rick, doesn't believe in belonging to a fraternity, and chose home life over living in the dorm or renting a cheap apartment. Those facts alone say a great deal about Big R, as I refer to him. Having an older brother seems to be an advantage for most girls – there is always the chance one of their friends will show an interest in a younger sister – but my brother has never brought home anyone even remotely interesting. On top of this lack of promising friends, Big R has never been in trouble with the police, has never been involved with an unsuitable partner with children from a previous marriage, has never embraced a new religion, or had a sexual crisis. All of the above seem to happen to my friends' siblings fairly regularly, and their homes are alive with electrical tension and the rush of knowing there may be some sort of emotional upheaval at any given time.

It's hard to imagine any kind of raw emotion bouncing around the energy-draining beigeness of our house. Everything in the whole place matches everything else, in varying shades of browns and golds, from drapes to wall-to-wall carpets to furniture. I would love to come home one day and find a bizarre abstract painting on the wall over the couch, or an unusual decorative object on the coffee table. A bibelot. I love that word, but it rarely comes up in conversation.

But even as I hate the drab state of my home and family, I have to admit, sadly, that I also fall into the same category. This is who I am; this is Rebecca Olchowecki:

My looks can only be described as passable. I'm not exactly short, but not tall, either. I'm neither heavy nor slender, my eyesight is good, my teeth fairly straight, and my skin just acts up for a few days a month, right before my period. I can't even take comfort in dreaming of some remarkable metamorphosis – a shining beauty emerging after one summer, sans glasses and braces and with old weight lost or new curves acquired.

While I never tripped over my own feet at track or slapped at the volleyball with open palms, I still wasn't good enough to make the second cut on any of the school teams. My grades have always been respectable, but I would never bring any honor to the school with my prowess on the debating team. I am far too inhibited to try out for the drama club, although I did joyfully raise my voice from the anonymity of the choir's large contralto section for an operetta last spring.

I haven't been totally dateless. A few boys from school have taken me out, but they certainly never tried to convince me to do anything that was slightly thrilling and maybe just the tiniest bit wicked. I noticed, more than once in fact, that by the end of the evening they seemed more uncomfortable than I did, hurrying away with a joke or an awkward attempt at a pecking sort of kiss. It was as if they sensed the dullness that surrounded me and were afraid that if they got too close, it would seep into them by osmosis. They were always polite after those indifferent dates, making small talk in class or in the line-up in the cafeteria, but I could see their eyes drifting away from mine, searching over my shoulder or the top of my head, as we discussed the unfairness of the day's home-work assignment or the state of Tuesday's lasagna. I knew they were looking for greener, more interesting pastures, wanting me to realize that, while they thought I was a nice girl, I wasn't to misinterpret their friendliness.

One morning I realized, with an unpleasant jolt, that, like the tortoise, I was simply slow and steady. I'd get there, wherever it was that I was headed, but with no amazing burst of glory or accomplishments worthy of media attention. I would just plod through the rest of my teenage years, never failing, but never really succeeding. It was such a dismal thought that I swore that, by the end of the school year, I'd change the course of my life.

I just wanted a little bit. I thought I'd be satisfied with something small. After all, I was that kind of person, used to doing small insignificant things, staying in the back-ground most of the time. But then something happened, without any preconceived plan. It was just a slip of the tongue. And what followed made me realize that I wanted a whole lot more than a little bit of anything.

We were sitting on the bleachers in the gym, waiting for the basketball tournament to start. It was Lauren, Katelyn, Mara, and me. We're friends, and we hang out together, but I can't really say that any of us are best friends. Each one of us more or less depends on the others to go places with and to be a shoulder to cry on. Occasionally one of us has a date, but there are always at least three of us looking for something to do each weekend. We just try to be there for each other. I don't know if girls everywhere do it, but it works for us, this unspoken pact between the less-than-popular girls that never lets one of us feel too alone, too out of things.

Lauren was talking. "You know my cousin Alexander, the one in Sin Men?"

We all groaned. How could we forget good old Alexander? Although we had never seen his group, Lauren gave us weekly updates about the great new Toronto hot spots where her cousin's band was appearing. Since none of us would probably ever get that far east in the next few years, there wasn't much chance of us actually catching Alexander or his spectacular drumming.

"Well," Lauren said, ignoring our expressions, "Sin Men is going to be on MuchMusic next weekend!"

"Really?" Katelyn asked, her face getting a pinched, suspicious look. I felt my features narrowing, too.

"Really. Swear. I swear it." Lauren slapped her hand to her chest, then took it off. "Well, they're *supposed* to be on. It all depends on some network timing thing. But if they are, Jessica Jann will be interviewing them on Saturday night's show. My aunt phoned my mom last night and told her."

We were all sick of Lauren's bragging about Sin Men and how they were always rubbing shoulders with big name bands and were always on the verge of cutting a recording deal – except every deal fell through because Sin Men didn't like this or that clause in the contract. It was just getting to be too much.

I was in a particularly bad mood. Just before I left the house my mother had declared, brightly, that we could spend Saturday together reorganizing my closet and dresser drawers. Even new shelf paper. She said it the way I imagine other mothers announcing a shopping spree at the mall.

I looked at Lauren, sitting there so smug and proud just because of her cousin. I wanted to make her feel as bad as I did. "Well, that can't be true," I said, "because Jessica Jann is my father's daughter from his first marriage, and I happen to know that she's going to be down in New York taping a special."

All three of the girls leaned forward and stared at me.

"Would you repeat that, please?" Mara said, her eyes bulging out in an unattractive way.

I licked my lips. I couldn't believe I'd said that about Jessica Jann. I couldn't believe I'd said anything. I wasn't a liar, I didn't even stretch the truth – at least not about anything important. I did sometimes tell little fibs to my parents, like adding a half hour on to how long I'd been doing my homework or saying I'd had a great time at a party when really I hadn't. But I was basically an honest person, the kind of person people believe. And I guess that's why I didn't know how to take the Jessica Jann lie back. When I thought about it later, I realized it would have been easy to shrug and laugh and say, "Just kidding." But I didn't.

"I said, Jessica Jann is my father's daughter from his first marriage, and –"

"But that means she's your sister!" Katelyn squealed. "Your half sister, Rebecca. Jessica Jann is your half sister! I can't believe it!"

They all pushed up against each other on the bleachers.

"Why didn't you say anything, Rebecca?" Lauren asked, shaking my arm. "You could have got Alexander a big break a long time ago, maybe last year."

"Shut up about Alexander, Lauren," Mara said. "We want to hear about Jessica. Have you met her, Rebecca? Does she ever . . ." Mara leaned farther forward, ". . . come to visit your dad?"

Suddenly there were loud cheers, whistles, and hoots, and we all looked down at our team as they jogged out onto the gym floor. Mara, Katelyn, and Lauren looked back at me. "Tell us, Rebecca, tell us what she's like,"

Katelyn shouted over the noise. A whistle blew and the crowd settled down.

"Let's get out of here," Lauren said. "Come on, Rebecca. Let's go somewhere where we can talk."

Nobody said anything on the way to the fast-food place near the school, but I practically had to run to keep up. It was as if they couldn't wait to hear everything, but didn't want me to start until we were seated. As if it were too important to discuss on the street. That gave me time to think something up.

When we finally had our food, Katelyn took a long slurp from her straw and said, "Now. Tell us everything."

No one had ever demanded that I tell them a thing. I was usually the listener, hearing everyone else's stories and making appropriate sounds of delight, horror, or envy. I wanted to prolong this moment.

I wiggled a french fry in the little white container of ketchup. "Well, my dad had this really brief marriage, ages ago," I started. "He was working in Toronto, and he met this woman and they got married. They had a baby, had . . . Jessica . . . but the marriage didn't work out. So my dad split and came here, and a few years later he met my mom. That's it. That's all there is." I took a deep breath. It was a logical enough story. It happened all the time.

"But why didn't you ever say anything before?" Lauren asked.

I noticed no one was eating except me. "It just never came up," I said, trying to sound casual.

"It never came *up*?!" Mara shrieked. "It never came up that you're related, very closely, to the queen of the VJ's at MuchMusic? To the person who talks to every hot group in Canada, not only backstage, but also in the dressing rooms? Rebecca! Jessica Jann is, like, an idol to a lot of people. How could you never mention it?"

I had a scary excited feeling, as if I were standing at the edge of a frozen river that had a sign that said THIN ICE, and I knew I was going to try to cross it anyway. My teeth kept mechanically grinding the cardboard fries. I crossed my arms on the table and leaned over them. I kept my voice low. "Look. It's like this. My dad doesn't really want people to know. He was kind of a jerk about it all, I guess. Left Jessica's mother, didn't send child support, that kind of thing.

"So he only confided it to me recently, you know, when he figured I was old enough to handle it. He told me right after we watched this TV show about people who need a lot of attention, glamor, adoration – sort of like Jessica – because something was lacking in their childhood, something important, like a parent."

Everyone nodded. It sounded as though I knew what I was talking about. And the TV show part was the truth. I had (alone) watched a talk show about attention-seeking adults one afternoon, when I was home from school with strep throat.

"It comes down to the fact that he doesn't really want anyone to know how irresponsible he was. He told me in the *strictest confidence*." I added that last part for security. Stories seem to sprout faster when they start as dark secrets. "So don't say anything, okay?"

Of course, three heads nodded.

Of course, by Monday, half the school knew.

The school corridor was busier than usual, with kids leaning up against the lockers and sitting cross-legged on the floor. I saw the small crowd as I turned the corner. "Here she comes," I heard someone say.

There was a sudden silence. I raised my chin and tried to look natural, even though my lips were trembling by the time I got to my locker. I could hear a rustling, restless moving, as if everyone was waiting for something to happen. I got my locker open, grabbed my books, took a deep breath, and turned around.

"Hey, Rebecca," Victor Muñoz called. "So what's she like? Is she as cool as she looks on TV?"

Victor Muñoz, the school's top jock, had never even acknowledged my existence before.

"Yeah, she's pretty cool," I said, as I slammed my locker shut. He was right beside me. I could smell him, hair gel with a tiny undercurrent of socks. I inhaled deeply.

Small murmurs ran through the crowd. "Did she ever take you backstage with her, Rebecca?" "How many times have you been to the set?" "Does she give you free

tickets to concerts?" I glanced at my watch, as if I had
somewhere to go, then smiled and started down the hall.
It was hard to walk away, especially from Victor, but I
wanted to take my time with my answers.

The quiet street my family lived on got busy over the next
few days. Cars filled with kids from school drove up and
down for hours, slowing as they passed the house.

"Seems to be a lot of traffic," my dad said, when he
came in from work. "I had to wait for three cars to go by
before I could even turn in to the driveway." He shook his
head. "I hope our street isn't getting to be some kind of
thoroughfare."

"Oh, I'm sure it's nothing, Mel," my mom said,
moving between the stove and the table with a platter
of Shake'n Bake chicken. "Probably just some minor
detour somewhere, diverting the cars down our street for
a day or two."

"I hope you're right," Dad said, taking the platter from
her and handing it to me. "Take a drumstick, Rebecca,"
he said. "I know what my little girl likes best."

As I took the drumstick, there was a passing blast of
music from outside. I gave the platter to my mother.

"You know, I noticed that most of those cars were filled
with teenagers," Dad remarked. I looked up, and he
smiled at me. "I'm so glad you're not that kind of girl,
Rebecca, joyriding in the streets, music blaring. Isn't this

much nicer, sitting down to supper together? Those kids out there don't know what a real family is all about."

A few evenings later, as I came out of my room to get a snack, I passed the living room and saw my mother. She was in her powder blue sweat suit, a towel draped around her neck and a pink sweatband holding her short dark curls away from her forehead, puffing away on her NordicTrack. As her arms and legs slid back and forth, she read the classifieds, which she folded on a little stand that was attached to the base of the skier.

"Anything, Mom?" I asked, stopping.

My mother gripped the ski poles and swung her arms more vigorously, her face an unflattering burgundy. "Not today," she said, gasping slightly. Even with the gasp, I recognized the slight tremor in her voice.

"Come on, Mom, you'll find something. But you really should take a computer course. It would definitely make you more marketable."

Mom's jaw jutted forward. "I'm too old to learn all that stuff. I have enough trouble figuring out Celsius and kilometers."

"You're not that old." Then, as Mom's face swung toward me, her eyes puffy and owlish behind the magnified lenses of her glasses, I changed it. "You're not old, Mom." I walked across the room to look out the front picture window. "I bet you could learn –" I quickly stepped back behind the drapes. A group of girls was standing across the street, taking pictures of our house.

The swishing of the skis stopped. "What are you looking at, dear?" Mom came up behind me. She stepped in front of the window, mopping her forehead with the towel. "Oh. Do you know those girls?"

I peeked around the edge of the curtain. "I think they go to my school."

"Now why would they be taking pictures of our house?"

I pulled my head back, ran my fingers up and down the edge of the drape, and raised one shoulder in half a shrug.

Mom put her hands on her hips. "Seems strange." Suddenly she threw her arm over her head and started waving to them, a big back-and-forth wave, as if she were signaling a ship.

"Mom! Stop! What are you doing?" I peeked again. The girls were talking to each other and pointing at the house. One started to cross the street.

"Just being friendly. Maybe they want to come over. You're not doing anything, are you, Rebecca? You could –"

I fumbled for the drapery cord and yanked on it, so the drapes swung shut, catching part of Mom's head. She clawed at the heavy brown material, stepping backward.

"Rebecca! Don't be so rude. They looked friendly."

"No. I have a lot of homework. And I don't even really

know them." I edged away from her, out of the room. "Please, Mom. Leave the drapes shut."

"Well, all right," she said, her brow furrowed. She started to disassemble the skier. "But when you see them at school, ask why they were taking pictures of our house."

"Right," I said, heading off toward my bedroom.

By Friday I had invitations to three parties for Saturday night. The crowded hallways at school opened as I passed through. There was a moment of reverent silence as I entered a classroom.

On Saturday afternoon I spent all the money I had on a long black velvet jacket, the kind Jessica often wore with jeans and a bustier on her Saturday night program. I *almost* got a hat like hers, but didn't want to overdo it. With my birthday money I planned to get some boots, black lizard, just like Jessica's. I had already seen them in the window of Buck's Saddlery.

On Saturday night I chose the party that sounded the most promising and got ready to go.

"I still don't know why you spent all your money on that one jacket," Mom said. "You could have got a couple of outfits from Valu-Mart with what you paid for that."

"I like it, Mom. It's cool."

Mom sniffed. "Since when is cool so important? Being neat, neat and clean, is what I've always stressed."

"Yes, Mom." It came out as a sigh. "See you later."

"Hold on, now. Your brother was kind enough to offer you a lift there, but how are you getting home?"

I smiled. "Don't worry. I'm sure I'll get a ride."

Michael Reznick from my chemistry class took me home. He parked outside my house and seemed really interested in what I had to say. Then, right in the middle of a sentence, he leaned over and kissed me, long and hard, as if he really meant it. It was my first *real* kiss, the first one with feeling. I liked it, but it made me think about what it would be like to kiss other guys. I knew I didn't have to limit myself to Michael, even though a week ago I would have given my right arm for a date with him. He asked me out for the next Saturday, but I had already promised another boy from the party, a cute guy called Serge, that I would go over to Mary Louise Mafee's place with him.

"Thanks anyway, Michael, but I'm busy," I said. I saw his face fall. I actually saw it. I always thought that was just an expression, but when I said no to Michael, all his features sort of slid downward, as if the muscles had given up. I, Rebecca Olchowecki, made a guy's face fall, a guy who had just given me this long, intimate, meaningful kiss. A surge of power ran through me. It was so strong that I was almost scared, but it also felt fabulous.

"Listen, it was really fun tonight. I mean it." I started to get out of the car, stopped, and said over my shoulder, "Maybe some other time. I'll be in touch." I slammed the door and walked toward my house. I'd always wanted to say that to someone.

The week flew by. One day I brought a picture of my dad to school. He was pretty young and was holding a baby girl (my cousin Elise). I put the photo in a Ziploc bag and passed it around, asking people not to take it out because it was special and I didn't want it to get too marked up. I didn't even say anything about who it was. People love to come to their own conclusions.

Another day I brought a little pair of my scuffed baby shoes. Same thing. The girls touched them gently, making aahing noises. The boys just looked at them, but I could tell they were dying to touch them, too.

Every day at lunch I had to decide where to sit. It seemed like everyone wanted me at their table. I had become one of the major suns in the great school solar system. The others, the many little moons and comets and stars, just sort of drifted around, out in the emptiness, hoping to be touched by a warming ray.

The story was growing, with a little help from me, but mainly all by itself. Like I said, stories germinate fastest when they start in the dark, but once they've got into the light, the best thing to do is to step back and leave them alone. This one was growing at breakneck speed. I let it.

What could it hurt?

*

Friday lunchtime. The cafeteria had that great hum of excitement at the promise of weekend possibilities and the relief of another week of school over. I was sitting at a table with Mary Louise Mafee and her friends. Mary Louise was talking about Saturday night.

"I'm so glad you're coming, Rebecca," she said. "Serge is really cool."

"Yeah. He seems okay."

"He and his girlfriend, this really snobby girl from St. Justine's, just broke up last month," a girl named Rhianne said. "They went out together for over four months and Serge was really bummed about the breakup. He hasn't taken anyone out since then. You're the first."

"He's in a band, too," Mary Louise added.

Why didn't that surprise me? I smiled brightly. "Really? Great."

Serge drove up at 8:30, right on time. As soon as I saw the car stop outside, I ran to the basement stairs and yelled down to my parents, who were sorting through holiday slides in the rec room.

"I'm going now. See you later."

"Don't be too late," I heard my father say. Suddenly his feet thumped up the stairs. I didn't think he'd come up. I opened the back door, trying to get outside before he got to the top of the stairs. I didn't want Serge to see him.

My dad's not abnormal looking or anything, but he definitely doesn't look like the kind of man who could have produced a daughter like Jessica Jann. Although genes are a tricky thing, and no one can prove anything by the size of a guy's ears or the fact that he's at least three inches shorter than his supposed famous daughter, I didn't want to take any chances. But I wasn't fast enough.

"Wait. Wait, Rebecca," Dad said, just as I was slipping out the screen door.

"What?"

"I'd like to meet this fellow. A father's prerogative, isn't it?" He gave a little chuckle. "The way the phone's been ringing lately, I'd say I'll be pretty busy, meeting all these boyfriends."

"Daaaaad."

"Come on, now. If he's a gentleman, he'll come to the door."

As if Serge had heard him, the doorbell chimed. Dad rubbed his hands together briskly and hurried from the back door to the front. He flung the door open with a flourish.

Serge looked down on him.

"Come in, young man, come in." Dad made a sweeping gesture with his arm.

"Dad, this is Serge. Serge, my father." My voice had a wooden robotic quality. I didn't want to leave any openings for discussion.

Serge grabbed my father's hand and pumped it up and down. "A real pleasure, Mr. Olchowecki. Everyone is very excited to learn about your daughter."

Dad looked at me, then back down at Serge's hand. "Well. Yes. We're real proud of our little girl, too, uh . . . Surge."

"Serge, Dad," I said. "S-E-R-G-E. You say Sairj."

"Do you see her often?" Serge asked, obviously not bothered by Dad's pronunciation of his name.

Dad looked at me again. He had this earnest look, the kind a dog gets when you're trying to teach it something and it knows there's a treat in it if it can figure out what you want. He made a little *heh-heh* sound, then looked back at Serge. "Guess you could say I do. As much as any father, I guess." His head turned back in my direction. "Don't I, Rebecca?"

I pushed between the two of them, breaking their hands apart. "Come on, Serge, let's go."

"You two have a good time."

I pulled at Serge's arm. He was looking at the living room, his eyes darting around as if he were trying to spot something. His eyes passed over my dad once more and I saw them taking in Dad's slightly stooped shoulders in his old checked sweater, his baggy pants, the threadbare plaid slippers.

We walked to the car in silence.

"He's not exactly what I imagined," Serge said, as we pulled away from the curb.

I forced a laugh. "Well, whose parents are?"

"Yeah. I guess."

Serge didn't have a lot more to say on the way over to

Mary Louise's, except to mention his band. "I play bass," he told me. "We've had a few gigs and we played in a band competition last month."

"Did you win?"

"Nah. It was rigged. One of the judges was the uncle of a guy in another band. Obviously they won."

"Too bad," I said. "What's your band called?"

"Scream of Love. Heard of it?"

"Uh, no. Not yet."

"Well, this time last year nobody had heard of Hot Spit either."

I still hadn't. I nodded.

"It was your sister who got them their start. They were knocking out crowds all over the West, but just couldn't get that break, you know. Just like us. But Jessica happened to be in Vancouver, caught them jamming at a club, and within a few weeks they had a mega contract. Right now they're over in Germany, booked solid for the next month. There's a big write-up about it in this month's *Rocking News*. Did you see it?"

I didn't want to appear totally out of it. "Oh, yeah. I think I read something about it."

"When do you think Jessica'll be coming to visit you next?" Serge asked, looking over at me.

I studied the billboard on my right. "She doesn't like me to tell people her schedule. You know how it is. She comes home to relax, just wants to lie low when she's here."

"I hear you." Serge nodded. "But listen, I'll give you our demo tape. Next time she's around, just slip it in, let her hear it without saying anything. Real casual. Get her reaction. Could you do that for me? Rebecca?"

My name sort of rolled off his lips. I liked the way he said it.

"Sure. Why not?"

There were twelve people at Mary Louise's. I was having a pretty good time with Serge when suddenly, at eleven o'clock, Mary Louise turned off the music.

"Okay, everyone, it's time!" she announced.

Everyone looked at me. "Time for what?" I asked. The whole room laughed as if I had said something funny.

"For Jessica's show, of course," Mary Louise replied. She turned on the TV, and everyone found a comfortable spot.

"Here she is. Look, she's got her hair different," Rhianne said. "I like it better down, like before."

"*Shhh*. Listen," someone scolded.

Jessica went in to her usual spiel, telling her viewers what was happening with the band scene around Canada. Her special guests were The Lasers. Then there were some taped dressing-room interviews and videos of the week's hits, from ten down to number one. Throughout the show Jessica was taking phone calls, reading notes, sending dedications out with songs.

"Sorry the switchboard gets so jammed, folks," Jessica

purred, "but it seems like *everyone* has a question for me. Be patient. I'll get to as many of you as I can."

"I tried to talk to her once," Eric said. He was Mary Louise's boyfriend. "I started dialing at the beginning of the show and they actually picked up my call. They put me on hold, with those little taped messages repeating every sixty seconds. I waited forty-five minutes – and don't forget, this is long distance to Toronto – then they told me they didn't have time for my question. My parents killed me when they got the bill. It took me over a month to pay it off. It's just a joke, this phoning thing. It's impossible to get through. I think they have it all set up beforehand, like taped calls or something."

"Yeah, the calls are probably screened," Mary Louise agreed. "How else could they get those requests ready so soon?"

"I could get through to her." I don't know why I said it. Nobody was asking me to.

"Could you? Right now?" Serge put his arm around my shoulders. "All right."

"Well, not right now. The show's almost over. But she always takes my calls, whenever I phone."

"Could some of us talk to her, if you tell her we're your friends?" Rhianne asked.

I shrugged. "I don't see why not." Everyone waited. "I'll call her at home this week and get something set up for next week's show."

Mary Louise clapped her hands. "Okay, everyone. One week from tonight. Back here, to talk to Jessica on the air. Right, Rebecca?"

"Right," I said. Serge's arm tightened around me. I was feeling so good that I was sure I could swing something. I had a whole seven days.

I had it worked out by Monday. Right after school I raced home and phoned the Toronto studio where Jessica's show was taped. The receptionist sounded bored, but said that, yes, they did take messages for Jessica, and if Jessica had the time, she would read it over the air.

"It's really *really* important," I said. "And it's just a few lines."

"It doesn't matter to me how long it is," the woman said. "I don't read 'em. I just stick 'em in her mailbag."

"Well, maybe you could write Urgent or something on the top. In red ink. To make her notice." There was silence. "Hello?" I said.

"Look, just give me the message, okay?"

I read what I had written. "Hi to Rebecca and all her friends, watching from that little hometown out west."

I could hear the tapping of her keyboard. "Okay," the woman said.

"Wait! Don't hang up. Could you . . . read it back to me?"

"Hi to Rebecca and all her little friends, watching from

that hometown out west." There was a touch of sarcasm in her voice.

"Good. Except it's not little friends, it's just friends. It's the hometown that's little. That little hometown out west. Or just leave out the little. It doesn't matter." I laughed, but it had an irritating shrillness, even to my own ears.

"Gotcha. Leave out little." There was more tapping. "Thank you for calling," she said mechanically, and there was a loud *click*, followed by the dial tone.

I phoned back on Thursday, praying it wouldn't be the same woman. It was a man this time.

"I left a message for Jessica Jann on Monday. I just wanted to make sure she got it. Is there any way I can –"

"I can't check on personal messages, but I can tell you that Jessica was in yesterday, and all her mail and messages were on her desk." The man's voice was kinder than the woman's.

"But you can't tell me if –"

"Sorry, I can't tell you anything for sure. But Jessica's pretty good about reading out as much as she can, and keeping in touch with her fans. She has a fan club. Would you like to join? I can mail you the information."

"No. That's okay. Thanks anyway." I hung up, feeling the first little bite of anxiety. Still, the worst that could happen was that she wouldn't read my message, and I could just make something else up. It was easy.

*

The same gang was at Mary Louise's on Saturday. As soon as Serge and I walked in, everyone crowded around me.

"So, what's happening? Will we get to talk to her?" Rhianne asked.

"I'm not sure. When I talked to her this week, she said it was true, all her calls *are* screened beforehand. She doesn't even have that much choice about who she talks to. But she might say hi to us or something." I thought that would be enough to hold them.

The show had only been on for about ten minutes when Jessica read my message. She actually read it. She was reading lots of other stuff from a stack of papers in front of her – dates for shows, requests, that kind of thing. Then she looked right into the camera, smiled, and said, "For Rebecca and all my fans out west. Hi, gang."

Everyone gave a sort of cheer and looked at me.

I shrugged. "Well, I guess that's all she was allowed to do this week." I reached for a nacho.

"I thought I'd get a chance to talk to her," Mary Louise said.

"I told you, Mary Louise, she doesn't have the final word," I said, dipping the nacho in some salsa. "You wouldn't believe how controlling the station managers are."

Mary Louise turned back to the TV, but a few minutes later she got up to go upstairs. I heard her say, "Be right back," to Eric.

I don't know how long she was gone, but it was near the end of the show, right after a commercial, when

Jessica pushed one of the buttons on the phone in front of her. "This is a good one, folks," she said. "Somebody's on the line who claims she's friends with my sister." A camera zoomed in on her face and her voice dropped a tone. "My phantom sister out in Alberta. Scary."

My body went cold. I saw my hand, which was reaching for my drink, stop in midair. It just stayed there, as if it didn't belong to me. I kept watching it, waiting for it to either take the glass or come back, but it didn't move.

Jessica smiled prettily at the camera and shook her head. "It's not that unusual, people claiming to be related to celebrities. You wouldn't believe the letters and pictures I get. A lot, I mean, *a lot*." She winked and let go of the button. "Hello," she said. "You're on the air. What's your story?"

"Hi, Jessica." The girl's voice was breathy, excited, unmistakable. "My name is Mary Louise Mafee and I'm best friends with Rebecca. We all just wanted to say hi to you and tell you how much we love your show. And you. Maybe you'll come out and do a show from our school the next time you're here to see Rebecca and your dad."

"*Whoa!*" Jessica said, her lips pursed and one eyebrow arched the tiniest bit. "Hold on there, Mary. Just who is this Rebecca?"

Mary Louise's voice dropped to a sort of whisper. "You know. *Rebecca*. Your *sister*."

"Sorry, sweetie. Some mistake. I don't go into too much personal stuff on the air, but let me tell you, I definitely haven't got a sister, and good old Pop won't be happy to hear he's got competition. Someone's feeding you a line. Now, have you got a video you'd like to see?" There was a loud buzz from the line. "No request? Well, we've just got time for the number three hit this week before our final interview. Catch you back."

Four jumping bodies filled the screen. I was able to force my hand back to my lap, but I didn't take my eyes off it. Nobody said anything. In a few seconds there were loud thumps on the stairs.

"Can you believe this? Did you guys see? What's going on, Rebecca?" Mary Louise demanded.

I looked up. Her eyes were catlike. Cruel. "It's a secret," I stammered. "She doesn't want to hurt her mother . . . her mother doesn't know she still sees Dad . . . I told Katelyn and Lauren and Mara . . . I . . ."

"Yeah. Right," Mary Louise said. "I go on national television and make a fool of myself, even tell my last name, all because you con us with some stupid lies. I can't believe we didn't see through you."

"No, I . . ." I turned to Serge. His arm wasn't around me anymore. He was staring at a bowl of popcorn on the table. I looked around at the rest of the faces, but they all looked like they had a few weeks ago. Perfect strangers.

Mary Louise picked up the remote and clicked off the television. The room was quiet, except for a few sounds – someone crunching on a nacho, the muffled gurgling of water running down a pipe between the walls, the far-off drone of a distant plane. There was one more sound, too, but this one only I could hear. It was the tiniest of noises. Just a little *poof.*

Probably the same one that old fishwife heard, too.

Sweet Bird of Youth

My Aunt Bev has to have a hysterectomy.

She phoned my mom with the news. The fact she actually telephoned meant that she was upset; she never calls. Because my mom's a soft touch, she said, "I'll drop over for a visit. Blake, too." I gagged when I heard that. The last place I wanted to go was Aunt Bev's. No self-respecting guy of fifteen wants to spend his Saturday afternoon visiting his aunt. Especially not one like Bev.

We're not even related anymore, in my opinion. My dad and Bev's husband were brothers. But they weren't like brothers at all. Or maybe it wasn't that they were so different, but that my mom and Bev are. I think my mom did good things for my dad, and Bev didn't do anything for Uncle Rod.

He left her when Toot was only five, and the only time I've seen him since was at my dad's funeral three years ago. He was drunk as usual, tried to pick a fight with Bev, then roared away in his beat-up Dodge, and I don't think anyone's heard from him again.

In the six years since he walked out, Bev and Toot just keep plugging along. Whenever my mom talks about them to me, she uses a fake cheery voice, but the truth comes out when Mom's sisters get together. Bev's name usually comes up in the whisper that people sometimes use, even when the person they're talking about is miles away. Maybe that's for my benefit, too. If they say catty things in a soft voice, it's not really mean. *Whisper, whisper, whisper. Beverly. Toot. That poor little Toot.* Mom doesn't say much, just supplies vague details on demand, but the others like a good story and pounce on any tidbit, grabbing it and carefully pulling it apart with the claws they usually keep hidden.

Toot. Can you imagine being eleven and having Toot for a name? My mom told me that when he was a baby, he had trouble with gas and was always ripping and roaring in his diapers. His dad called him a little tooter and the name just stuck. Besides his rotten name and a dad who never phones or writes, Toot's had to put up with the men following Bev as she moved every year, a different boyfriend for each apartment. Bev's skinny and laughs too loud and smokes two packs a day (Export 'A'), but she always had some different guy hanging around. *Until Jake.* He's been living with her for way over a year now; a record as far as Bev's concerned. "My common-law husband" is what she calls him. In a proud sort of way. I think "common-law" has a sleazy ring to it. Suits Jake.

A few times a year, Mom will invite Bev and Toot over. She makes a big meal and has a shopping bag full of my old clothes and books and toys for Toot. I never really know if he wants them or not; he's a strange kid and hardly ever looks at anyone or says much. Except to my mom.

She's really okay as far as mothers go. She's on my case a lot about unimportant stuff, like my hair and eating politely and not wearing torn jeans everywhere – the usual stuff – but underneath it all, she's all right. She can make anyone feel comfortable. Even Toot. Sometimes I'd walk into the kitchen, while Bev and whoever were hooting in the living room or out on the patio, and I'd hear Toot chirping away like a cricket on a still summer night. My mom would be smiling and nodding as she basted the turkey or tossed the salad. But as soon as Toot saw me, he'd quit talking; his mouth would snap shut and he'd put his head down and pick at the little scabby pieces of skin around his nails, or examine the ragged cuff on his sweatshirt as if he'd never seen it before. Then Mom would ask me to take Toot to my room and show him some of my science equipment or a new CD, but the kid never wanted to go.

We haven't seen Bev and Toot for quite a few months, and I've never been to their latest apartment. I tried to talk my way out of going for this visit, but Mom can always get me to do things by making me feel guilty. This guilt trip was about how Bev doesn't have any other family, having grown up in foster homes, and how much it means to her that Toot has a cousin. "Such a thoughtful cousin," were Mom's exact words. *Sure. As if Bev would call me thoughtful.* Then when we got there, Toot wasn't even home, just Bev, Aunt Beverly, sitting like some queen with her hair all piled up, wearing tons of makeup and a shiny silver jumpsuit, the kind women wore in the movies way back in the sixties. She said Toot had gone off on his bike; she told him to stay home but he never listened to her.

Jake was at the legion, having his usual Saturday afternoon session. I was glad he wasn't there. He was too friendly, laughing almost as loud as Bev and putting his arm around me. "Call me Uncle Jake, pal," he'd say every time I saw him. *No way.* He isn't my uncle, and I don't ever intend to be his pal. So I don't call him anything. I don't even really look at him after that time last Christmas. I never told anyone; after all, he's such a wimpy little geek that it didn't even scare me. I just pushed away his sweaty hand with the greasy fingernails (he works at the gas station on Kingsford Avenue) and said, "Drop dead, you jerk," in a quiet voice. Then he got all goofy, laughing and gulping his drink, slapping me on the back and calling me buddy. "Hey, buddy, it was a joke. Just a joke, buddy." I went upstairs and stayed in my room until they left.

*

This apartment was like all the rest. Hot, crowded, filled with furniture and fancy little glass things and millions of pictures in frames. I noticed one new thing right away. A metal birdcage on a table in front of the balcony doors. Inside the cage was a bright yellow canary. It was hopping around on its perch, jumping down to peck at seeds scattered on the newspaper at the bottom of the cage and admiring itself in the little plastic mirror attached to one side. I squatted down to have a better look.

"That's Toot's new pet," Bev said. "His first pet, really. We never had no animals before, too much trouble. But Toot's been makin' such a fuss lately, wants a dog. Course we can't have a dog in the apartment, so finally I gave in and said he could get a hamster or a bird. He brought that thing home a couple of months ago."

"What's its name?" I asked, putting a finger through the narrow bars. The little bird stopped its frenzied hopping and looked at my finger.

"Oh, I don't know. Toot never tells me anything." She waved her cigarette at the bird. "He just talks to that old thing all the time. He takes it in his room at night and I hear him whispering to it for ages. Sometimes Jake has to holler at him to shut up so we can get some sleep."

There was silence as we all looked at the canary, as if we were waiting to hear the secrets Toot told it. When I looked back at Bev, she had an odd look on her face, her mouth turned down. Almost sulky. "Can't think why he likes it so much. Never does nothing. Doesn't sing or talk or anything. Hope he remembers to feed it while I'm in the hospital."

I looked down at the tiny creature, imagining it lying on its back on the bare newspaper, stiff and cold, its scaled legs pointing upward toward the empty perch.

"How long do you think you'll be in?" my mom asked.

Bev stubbed out her cigarette with a jerk. "I dunno for sure. Hard to understand doctors. Could be a week – depends how everything goes once they open me up and get in there."

"What about Toot?" I think my mom feels responsible for Toot somehow. Sorry for him.

"Toot, that kid! He's been in a state since I told him. Doesn't even seem to care that I need the operation; doesn't ask me how I'm feeling or anything, just doesn't want me to go to the hospital. He doesn't like staying home in the evening if I'm not here. I don't know why. Big baby's what I call him. Eleven years old and still a mamma's boy."

I stood very still, my finger wedged tightly between the bars of the cage.

"I just tell him he's darn lucky Jake's around. Lotsa kids his age would end up sittin' alone, but he's got Jake. And Jake's good to him." She seemed to be talking louder and faster, like she was ready for an argument. "Last week he brought home one of those GameBoys for Toot. Them things cost over a hundred bucks, you know. And that kid didn't even want it. Wouldn't even take it out of the box. Spoiled brat."

There was the sharp scratch of a match being lit, and then the harsh sound of Bev's breath as she dragged hard on the cigarette. The bird swiveled its yellow head to one side, listening. After a long minute, I heard the soft sigh of smoke being blown out.

"Kids, eh? Never know when they got it good."

My finger seemed stuck. I couldn't push away the feeling that had started when Bev was talking about going to the hospital. It was a sudden cold scared feeling, an ashamed feeling, like when you know you failed a test and the teacher starts reading out the scores, highest to lowest. You know you'll be the last on the list, and you know there's no way you can change what's going to happen. I tried not to think of the feel of Jake's hot hand.

"Mom," I said, still not turning around, "maybe Toot could stay with us while Bev's in the hospital. We've got lots of room. He could bring the bird."

There was only a second's hesitation. "Why not? He's no trouble, Bev. Let him come. I can drop him off at school on my way to work, and he can take the bus back afterward. Just until you're home and feeling better." My mom's voice had a surprised sound, a what-a-good-idea sound, as if she had just thought of it herself.

There was a sudden flapping flurry in the cage. Bev

came up behind me and looked over my shoulder. Her smell was strong, perfume and stale smoke.

"Well, would you look at that!"

I followed her gaze to the weightless creature sitting on my rigid finger, staring up at me with its tiny dull black eye-bead.

"That stupid bird never hopped on no one's finger before." She squeezed my shoulder, hard. "Whaddya know, eh kid?"

Pas Seul

*I*nez surveys the sand surrounding her. It's pure white, each grain smaller than a granule of salt. The heat shimmers off the surface in tiny waves that she can only see out of the corner of her eye.

She picks up a handful of the searing white silk and lets it fall through her fingers, tilting her head back and staring into the unbearable blue of the Caribbean sky. It is hard to believe that, in the next few hours, this cloudless brilliant color will transform itself into an inky velvet curtain casually pinned with stars.

Inez feels a thump of pleasure deep under her ribs and lays back on her woven mat. The air blows across the island, as it has every afternoon for the last four days, with such a tangible presence that she can almost feel it settle on her skin. She waits for the caressing breath to soothe the hot stinging rawness of her shoulders, her knees, and her shins. She has been in the sun too long today; she knows the pain will intensify by tonight. She will wait for the stiffness, the skin stretched so taut that it feels as though it might split open if touched, like a tomato yielding to a sharp knife. She will welcome the pain. The physical ache will remind her that she is unhappy.

Inez stops breathing as the woman on the thick hotel towel beside her stirs and sits up. The woman reaches for her tube of sunscreen and begins to apply it to her shoulders and arms. As she rubs busily, Inez watches from behind her sunglasses, seeing the freckled shoulders, the loose skin buckling over the elbows, the thick untidy waist.

Without turning, the woman calls, "Inez, honey, can you put some of this stuff on my back?"

Inez remains motionless, feigning sleep, her hands uncurled and defenceless on the tops of her thighs. She doesn't want to let her fingers touch the slightly rounded shoulders, or to run her greased palms over the soft back.

When Marion's all dressed up, she can still look good, looks younger, in fact, than the mothers of most of Inez's friends. Inez knows how hard her mother works at it – spending hours on her hair and skin, constantly dieting, joining one health club and then another, buying exercise videos to use at home. But when Marion puts on a skimpy bathing suit and has the sun on her face, she is still forty.

Inez hopes that what she read recently in a magazine at the dentist's office isn't true, that she won't end up with a figure similar to her mother's. The article stated that a prospective husband need only look at his future mother-in-law to see what lay ahead.

When Marion looks over her shoulder, Inez closes her eyes, even though they're invisible behind the reflective silver sunglasses she bought in the hotel gift shop.

"I can't get over how much you look like I used to," Marion says. A flash of panic touches Inez. Can her mother pick up her thoughts? Marion continues, ignoring Inez's lack of response. "Slim legs, long neck, strong straight back. A true dancer's body." Her sigh is heavy. "I hope you'll reconsider, Inez. You have such talent. I was always sorry someone hadn't pushed me a little harder. All my dance teachers, even the dance master at the Academy, said I showed real promise. But I didn't have the ambition, didn't have the energy you have. I've always envied your ability to focus."

Inez keeps her breath deep and even, so her chest rises and falls smoothly. It's easier to pretend that she's asleep and can't hear. She hates when her mother tries to woo her out of her silence. Her mother doesn't even seem aware that she's the one who creates the constant tension that hovers around Inez like a swarm of hornets.

Inez knows she isn't moody or temperamental – words her mother has lately used to describe her – she's just angry, partly at her mother's constant nagging, which is always carefully hidden under put-on cheeriness. But most of all, Inez is angry at herself. She had been so sure about the future. About her own ability. Her mother had encouraged her all these years, told her she could do anything she wanted. Told her she could be the best. But obviously she isn't.

She might be good enough for the corps, but not good enough to be chosen as a principal dancer. Although she never would have confessed it to anyone, she had thought there was a chance. More than a chance. She had thought she would be chosen. Then came the audition, where she'd danced better than she thought possible, had felt herself almost leaving her body, dancing and dancing with a kind of freedom that she'd never experienced before. And then the crushing words, the "we wish we could have picked all of you, the decision was so difficult, you're all so excellent, *blah blah blah*." Lies.

And now she can't bear to think about another year of practice, another year of waiting, wondering if she'll be good enough the next time around. The thought of trying and then failing again starts a hot throbbing in her temples.

It would be easier not to try. Before they came on the trip, she decided there wouldn't be a next year, not for her. She was finished as a dancer.

Hearing Marion's second sigh, a tiny rustle, and then silence, Inez lets a sliver of light in under one eyelid. Marion is lying on her stomach, her head turned away from Inez, a shirt covering her hair from the sun's fading

power. From the sigh, Inez knows Marion's mouth is
stitched into its usual tight irritated knot. Silently, the girl
gets to her feet and steps away from her mat, glancing at
her mother's inert body.

"Honey?"

Inez freezes. Marion's head is still turned away.

"I'm sorry if this is boring for you. Being stuck here
with me."

Inez draws a circle in the sand with her big toe. "No,
Mom. It's not boring. It's so peaceful here. Relaxing." She
hadn't meant to say that, but it was true. The words just
came out.

"I thought there might be more people your own age
here, more for you to do." Marion's voice is muffled by
the shirt and the slight breeze. "I hoped you would have
some fun, have some time to think about . . . things.
What you want to do." Inez draws a second ring around
the first one and stares at it. "I only want you to do what
makes you happy. You know that, Inez."

When her mother doesn't say anything more, Inez
softly pads away. She walks down the beach, her feet
splashing in the soft white curl of foam licking at the
pliant sand, and she watches the tiny crab holes filling
and popping open with the push and pull of the water.

She hadn't wanted to come on this holiday, hadn't
wanted to leave the comfort of her room and everything
that was familiar. Ever since the audition she hadn't gone
to her dance classes, or even used the barre her mother

had installed in her bedroom, except as something to throw clothes over. She hadn't wanted to do anything. She knew her mother had booked the trip to cheer her up, drag her out of her deep hole of self-pity. But Marion would never admit that. No, Marion had sprung the trip on Inez as a surprise, saying it was an early birthday gift. Inez didn't even want to think about the begging and borrowing Marion must have done to come up with the money.

"All my life I've dreamed of going to the Caribbean," Marion had told her, holding up the plane tickets with a flourish, "and it's finally come true. Isn't it wonderful? Aren't you excited? Just imagine us, for a whole week, on a beautiful island in the middle of the ocean."

Inez had arranged her face in the appropriate expression of pleased gratitude. "Sure, Mom. It sounds fabulous. Great." *Except that it's your dream again, not mine*, she thought. *You're giving me your dream for my birthday. Happy birthday to you, Mom.*

As Inez walks along the sand, she looks down, watching her legs and feet. The calf muscles tense and release, tense and release. She wonders how long it will take for her calves to become smaller and softer; how long before her toes repair themselves. She can't remember the time when her toes looked normal. It would have been long before she started wearing pointe shoes.

A little way down the beach past the hotel holiday crowd, where the strip of sand between the palms and the water narrows, Inez stops to watch a pelican swooping lazily just offshore. Looking up to admire the graceful gliding of the huge bird, she automatically begins to press her feet against the sand. First position, then second, up to fifth. She surprises herself as she leans toward the water in a sudden arabesque, one arm reaching forward, the other extended behind. Just as she starts to lift her leg to follow the horizontal line of her body, she stops, rearranges her feet, forces them to be still. She tries to stand casually, let her toes loosen, her spine curl. Reminds herself she's done with arabesques.

The pelican circles over her one more time, then drops heavily, awkwardly, into the quiet surface of the water. It seems to be dive-bombing recklessly; a kamikaze pelican. It disappears under the water, but emerges almost immediately, a gleaming fish flipping in its beak.

Inez watches the flash of the sun on the fish. *Poisson*, she thinks. *Pas de poisson*, the fish step. She crosses her feet back into fifth, rising on her toes, head lifted, back arched. She imagines one of the boys from class – maybe Stefan, he has delicate but strong fingers, yes, Stefan – putting his hands around her waist and lifting her, easily, in a *pas de poisson*.

The bird flaps its huge wings slowly, farther out over the ocean, its composure restored, graceful again.

"Gots him a good one," says a voice behind Inez.

Inez drops her heels and turns around. The speaker is an old woman. Inez can't tell just how old she is, but she's

old. Her hair is short and grizzled under a torn straw hat.
Her eyes seem to have no color, as if the sunlight has
drained them. "A good one," she repeats.

"Yes," Inez says, looking from the woman to the dis-
appearing pelican. She glances back at the woman.
Warily.

Most of the islanders are reserved. They're courteous,
but in a watchful manner. They never ask questions,
almost never start a conversation. This woman's voice has
the same aloof dignity Inez has heard in the men and
women who work at the hotel or in the small shops in the
village. But her face, the warm mocha skin leathery and
crisscrossed with lines, has a certain curiosity – a lively
expression – in spite of her age. She is leaning up against
the hairy bark of a palm tree with a short straight stick in
one hand, and she is surrounded by a small herd of skinny
jostling goats. Inez wonders why she didn't see her there
as she came up the beach.

The old woman makes a sound in the back of her throat
as the goats bump against her legs, and they momentar-
ily stop their milling and stand as if waiting. Then the
woman puts her hands on the flat heads of the two goats
closest to her. The pushing starts again.

Inez looks around. She sees how far she is from the
hotel, and remembers her mother's warnings. She thinks
about how she must look to this old woman – a sun-
burned girl with long blonde hair, a pink-and-scarlet
bathing suit, silver sunglasses – dancing alone. She opens

her mouth, hesitates, then tells herself she's silly. After all, it's just some ancient crone.

"I was . . . sort of, well, dancing." The old head nods, the loose brim of the hat flapping up and down. "I've been going to ballet practice for as long as I can remember. Most of my life, I guess," Inez says. Her voice grows louder. "But I'm not really a dancer."

As a sudden strong wave splashes up against Inez's shins, she takes a step up the beach, toward the woman and the goats. The goats' heads swing in her direction, their strange ocher eyes expressionless but mildly alarming. Inez steps back into the water.

"I've always wanted to be one. But about all I do is practice. I don't really think I'll get there." She watches one goat wander away from the others and nibble at a low bushy plant spreading out onto the sand. "Just a silly dream, I guess."

The woman reaches over and taps the goat's side with the stick. The goat moves away from the plant, its mouth still chewing. The woman looks up at Inez and chuckles. One of her front teeth is missing. Inez can't be certain if there are any teeth on the bottom, but from the way the jaw protrudes and the bottom lip is sucked inward, she decides there aren't. The woman smacks her lips to stop the chuckling.

Inez smiles uncertainly, and brushes away a strand of hair blown into her lip gloss by the wind. There is a sudden commotion of wind and waves. Inez shivers, crossing her arms over her chest.

"You're a dancer, all right," the woman says. Then, "Sun going down." Without waiting for a reply, she starts walking, her long skirt flapping out behind her. She taps her leg with the stick and the goats trot around her.

Inez lifts her hand in a wave, even though the old woman isn't looking back. She stares after the woman and the animals until they veer off the beach into the bush. Then she turns, steps out of the water, and walks toward the hotel on the damp, packed sand.

The last sunbathers have left. Inez starts to run along the deserted beach with the light out-turned step that is the only one she knows now. Ahead of her she can see the small lonely figure of her mother sitting up on the towel, her hand shading her eyes against the final dazzle of sun on water as she looks down the beach.

Inez stops, watching her mother watching her. She poises, then *pliés*, her body dipping. Extending a leg, toe pointed, she twirls clockwise on the hardened sand, full circle. As she finishes the *fouetté* with a spinning stop in fourth position, one foot in front and parallel to the other, her arms reach overhead. The reddened skin between her shoulder blades and on the tops of her arms crinkles and stings. Then, as her arms continue upward, she feels something give way with an almost audible snap. A release. She closes her eyes.

She stands motionless, allowing the pain of her scorched skin to mix with the comforting familiarity of the pose. For that instant Inez thinks of a butterfly. She knows it's a silly predictable thought, the butterfly emerging from the cocoon, but she doesn't push it away.

She remains in position and lets the joy of her *fouetté* sink in. After a long moment she opens her eyes and looks toward her mother.

Marion is unmoving. Then, slowly, she brings her hands together, over and over again, and the clapping, soundless in its distance, falls around Inez, warmer than the last rays of the Caribbean sun.

Shasta

On the second day of school the students were assigned tables in biology, and Hayley realized she'd seen Shasta before. The girl hadn't been in any of her classes last year, but Hayley had a shadowy recollection of someone who could have been Shasta in the cafeteria, or the library, or maybe just somewhere in one of the many hallways of the huge school.

A lot of the classes were larger than usual. The school had had to make the eight grade ten classes into seven grade elevens, partly because of staff cuts, partly because of space. Mr. Treglov, the biology teacher, called out the students' surnames in alphabetical order, putting the first four people at table one, the second four at table two, and so on. Hayley was second last to be called. As she pushed her way through the bodies milling around the crowded room, she heard Mr. Treglov call out one more name.

"Zacharie, Shasta. Table twelve."

"Hi," Hayley said.

The girl set her books on the table, then peeked around the shiny hair covering part of her face. "Hi," she said back, in not quite a whisper, but her voice so low that Hayley could hardly hear it.

Mr. Treglov started right in with his plans for the first lab assignment, the old frog dissection. There were the usual groans and exaggerated gagging.

"But Mr. T., we did that back in middle school," a boy at the table in front of Hayley called out.

"You are to be commended on your memory, Mr. . . . ." Mr. Treglov checked his seating plan. "Mr. Whelan. Yes, most of you will have already done work with this lowly vertebrate. It's just a starting point, something familiar to begin the year. Is it a worry to you, Mr. Whelan, the thought of touching amphibian flesh?"

The whole class laughed. Hayley thought she was going to like Mr. Treglov. He was strict and old-fashioned in a way, but seemed naturally funny. Not like some of the teachers, who tried too hard to act the same age as their students, only emphasizing the hopeless chasm between them.

After Mr. Treglov filled them in on what to expect the next day, he handed out the cutting chart. Just before the bell, he added that anyone absent from the following biology class without a doctor's note would be called upon to do the dissection whenever they next showed up in class. "Your spotted friend will be waiting for you, for as long as it takes you to return to class. Just let me say this. A leopard frog, once deceased, does not do well sitting in its dissecting pan for too long. You may as well get it over with, ladies and gentlemen. A dead frog, unlike a fine wine or a woman, does not grow more interesting with age."

It was a passable joke. No point deductions. Hayley smiled at Shasta, waiting for her to comment on the teacher's remark, but Shasta was looking down at the open binder on her lap, her pen still poised over the sheet. Hayley saw that she had drawn a frog. It looked just like the pictures on the chart Mr. Treglov handed out.

"Don't forget to wear your apron tomorrow," Hayley said. She gathered up her books and slid off the high stool. "Ugh. I hate the thought of it."

Shasta looked at her for the first time, and her lips lifted in the tiniest smile. "I'll do it," she said in a low raspy voice that made Hayley lean closer to her.

"You'll do the whole thing?"

Shasta nodded. "I don't mind frogs. We used to eat frog legs for supper a lot. Before we moved up here." Her voice had a lilt to it, not quite an accent, but something different. *French?* Hayley wondered. *But no, that's not it.*

Hayley half smiled at Shasta. She didn't know whether the other girl was making fun of her or telling the truth. But, in thinking about cutting open the frog tomorrow, she hoped Shasta wasn't the type to make things up.

*

The next morning, as soon as they were at their table, Shasta studied the diagrams on the dissecting chart, then deftly pinned the frog down and picked up the forceps with her left hand. Lifting the thin skin of the frog's abdomen, she took the scalpel in her right hand and made a shallow cut. Before Hayley could even move close enough to see what she was doing, Shasta had inserted the rounded edge of her scissors into the incision and was cutting the frog's belly open. Then she made a quick lateral slash across the small chest.

"Slow down," Hayley whispered, holding her own scalpel over the spread-eagled form. "We can't finish too fast. And when Treglov heads over here, let's try to make it look as if we're in this thing together."

Shasta glanced toward the teacher, then pushed up the sleeves of her shirt. "Okay." She looked at Hayley. "If you want to do something, roll back the skin I just cut free."

Holding her breath, Hayley gingerly plucked the fragile skin away with her forceps so that Shasta could pin it in place. By the time Mr. Treglov walked by their lab table, Shasta was cutting through the muscular body wall, exposing the internal organs.

"Good, Miss Zacharie, Miss Yaskiw. Good. It's nice to have one team who isn't afraid of a little surgery. Keep up the nice work, ladies."

After the period Hayley and Shasta walked down the hall together. "Did you really eat frog legs, Shasta?"

"Yeah. They're pretty common where I grew up. My granny dipped them in flour and salt and pepper and then fried them with green onion, some lemon juice, and if we had them, mushrooms. Then she sprinkled some parsley on top. They taste delicious, sort of like . . ." She thought for a second, then shrugged. "Well, I can't really describe the taste."

Hayley looked down at Shasta. She was quite a bit shorter than Hayley, but had a full soft body. Her long black hair hung halfway down her back. She wasn't exactly pretty, but there was something about her face that made Hayley want to look at her. *Exotic*, Hayley thought. *She looks exotic.* "Fishy?" she asked.

"What?"

"The frog legs. Do they have a fishy taste?"

Shasta shook her head. "Not the ones we caught in the lake. Some of the little kids, they'd catch them at the edge of the bayou, where the water was swampy. I wouldn't eat those." She walked along, her eyes fixed on something far down the hall. "But we didn't always fry the legs. Granny would cut them up and throw them into gumbo, too."

"Isn't gumbo some kind of stew?"

"Sort of. But the gumbo we eat is more soupy than a stew. It always contains something from the water, but you can add almost anything else you like. Lots of vegetables – tomatoes, beet tops, okra."

Hayley nodded. She felt too stupid to ask what okra was. She'd look it up in the dictionary. Okra and bayou.

"Hayley! Hey, Halo!"

Hayley touched her lips, to assure herself that her lipstick was still shiny, then turned around, smiling.

"Hi, Jarret." She stood on tiptoe to kiss a thin blond boy on the cheek.

"How's it going? Do your frog thing?"

"Yeah. It was *so* icky." She delicately wrinkled her nose. "I hate all that biology stuff. Oh. Hi, Ryan." Hayley's voice dropped when she saw who was behind Jarret.

"Hey, Hayley. And hello. Introduce me to your friend, Hayley."

Hayley rolled her eyes at Jarret, then turned to Shasta. Shasta was staring up at Ryan, gripping her books tightly against her chest. Her nostrils flared slightly, as if she were taking a deep breath and getting ready to run.

"This is Shasta," Hayley said. "Shasta, Ryan and my boyfriend, Jarret." She put her hand on Jarret's arm.

Jarret smiled and said hi, but Ryan bowed stiffly from the waist. "Shasta," he said, his mouth slowly curling upward. "My pleasure."

"Don't mind him," Hayley said. "He watches too many old movies."

Shasta didn't seem to hear her. She was still looking up at Ryan. Her wide dark eyes, rimmed in a thin line of black, were huge. Hayley hadn't really noticed Shasta's eyes before.

"Small dilemma about the party tomorrow night,

Halo," Jarret said. "My mom needs to use my car. Hers is in the shop this week."

Hayley raised one shoulder. "No problem. I'll get my dad's."

"The Audi? He'll never let you borrow it, will he?"

"Like I said, Jarret, no problem."

A buzzer sounded overhead. "Great, Halo. You have a break now?" Jarret asked.

"I wish. I've got trig." She turned around to ask Shasta what class she had, but the girl was gone. Hayley looked up and down the crowded hall, but Shasta had disappeared in the crush of bodies hurrying to class.

"She isn't exactly your type, is she, Hayley?" Ryan asked. He was looking down the hall, too. "Not one of the usual Hayley fans."

"Shut up, Ryan." She narrowed her eyes and gave an exaggerated pout to her lips. "Just shut up."

Jarret put his arm around her and pulled her against him. "Who wouldn't love such a sweetheart?"

"Yeah, yeah," Ryan said. "But seriously, Hayley, how do you know her? Shasta."

"She's in my biology class. Lab partner."

"Lucky you," Ryan said. Hayley couldn't tell if he was being sarcastic or meant it.

On Monday morning Hayley was hanging up her jacket when she overheard two guys a few lockers down from hers. "Hey, look, she's got a tail today."

Hayley looked up to see who they were talking about. She followed their gaze to the other side of the hall. Shasta was walking by, her hair in one gleaming braid down her back. It wasn't an ordinary braid, or even a French braid. The hair was twisted and woven in a beautifully intricate detail that Hayley had never seen.

One of the boys snickered. "Makes her easier to ride. Something to hold on to so you don't fall off."

Hayley watched Shasta. She didn't look around or change her expression, so Hayley didn't think she'd heard the strange conversation. But later that morning, when Shasta came into biology, Hayley saw that the braid was undone, only a few waves left to show it had ever been there.

They didn't do another experiment in biology for the next two weeks, instead spending each class watching slides and videos, or copying notes. Hayley didn't say much to Shasta. For the first two classes after the frog experiment she had stood by the table when class was over, half waiting for Shasta. But Shasta always had her head down and didn't seem to notice. After those two times Hayley didn't bother, just hurried out as soon as the bell sounded, catching up with her friends or meeting Jarret for lunch.

At the end of September, as Jarret was driving Hayley home from school, he mentioned Shasta.

"You know that girl you were with in the hall one day? The little one with the weird name?"

"Shasta?"

"Yeah, Shasta. Ryan wants to take her out."

"Ryan? Please."

"What's wrong?"

"Ryan is such a phony. You know I can't stand him. And why would he want to go out with Shasta? She's definitely not the sort of girl Ryan usually takes out. She practically jumps when anyone looks at her."

Jarret shrugged. "He came up to me yesterday after practice and asked if you could set something up with her."

Hayley suddenly remembered the look on Shasta's face when she met Ryan. It could have been pure nervousness, or it could have been that rush that starts things happening in your head and body when you connect with someone.

"Well, I guess I could ask her. Maybe she sees something in Ryan that I don't. He's good-looking enough, but that's all there is." She slid across the seat and put her hand on Jarret's leg. "He's just not my type. I like a guy with a brain and charisma. *And* incredible looks."

Jarret eased the car to a stop at a red light and put his arm around Hayley's shoulders, pressing his lips against her hair. Hayley looked up at him, letting her lips part slightly, and he leaned down and kissed her. The kiss went on until the light turned green and there was a *toot* from the car behind them. With a slight groan, Jarret pulled his mouth away from Hayley's and started driving again.

"Anyway, Ryan and I were talking, Halo."

"Yeah?"

"I don't think it's such a good idea for you to, you know, hang out with Shasta."

"What are you talking about?" Hayley opened her purse and took out a lipstick. Stretching forward, she studied her face in the rearview mirror, touched the lipstick to her lips, and put it back in her purse. She fluffed up her bangs, then sat back. "First of all, I don't hang out with her. She's just in one of my classes."

"I know, but if you even walk with her between classes, people see you together. It's . . . I just heard some stuff that's going around. One of the guys heard it from the quarterback on the Wallis team."

"What kind of stuff?"

"Just, like, well . . . she'll make it with practically anyone."

Hayley laughed. "Get serious, Jarret. You've seen her. She's so shy it almost hurts to look at her. It's just some stupid locker-room talk. And probably the reason for Ryan's interest. What a worm."

Jarret looked over at her. "You don't really know her though, do you?"

"No. But neither do you."

"I know what I hear, Hayley." He smiled at her. Jarret's

smile usually made Hayley go all soft inside. Today it irritated her.

"Well, you shouldn't believe everything one of your jock buddies tells you." She moved back across the seat to the door. "In my opinion, if Shasta goes out with Ryan, she's dating beneath herself. And," she paused for a moment, "maybe it's not such a good idea for *you* to hang around with Ryan. I wouldn't want anyone thinking you share anything – like brain size, for example."

"Touché." Jarret didn't say anything more for the next kilometer or so. "Look. Whatever we think about Ryan or Shasta, the point is, if they want to get together, they can. It has nothing to do with us."

"Right," Hayley agreed.

Hayley asked Shasta about double-dating the next day after biology class. "Ryan asked me to set it up, Shasta. What do you think? We could go to a movie or something."

Shasta's face was tight, expressionless. Then she blinked and shook her head. "Is this for real, Hayley? He really wants to go out with me? Or is it a joke?"

"Why would it be a joke?"

Shasta shrugged.

"Look, it's not a joke. So do you want to or not?" As she asked the question, Hayley realized she wanted Shasta to say no, I already have a boyfriend, or just no, I don't think so.

"All right." The tightness on Shasta's face shifted the tiniest bit. "First I'll have to make sure it's okay with my grandmother. She can be sort of strict."

Hayley wrote down her phone number. "Call me tonight. I'll be talking to Jarret and he can tell Ryan." She handed the paper to Shasta. As Shasta took it, Hayley could see that her fingers were shaking.

On Friday night, when Jarret picked Hayley up, Ryan leaned forward from the backseat.

"Hey, you get her address?"

"Of course. Way out on Addis, at the very end. But you could have called her yourself, Ryan. Pretty low-class, don't you think?" She didn't wait for an answer. "Which movie are we going to, Jarret?"

Jarret shifted into third. "My parents went out to a wedding or something. They're gonna be pretty late. We thought we'd just pick up a couple of videos and hang out at my place tonight, okay?"

Hayley folded her arms over her chest and shrugged. "I guess so. But I told Shasta we were going out."

"We are, Hayley," Ryan said. "We're going out to Jarret's house. We'll have a little party, just the four of us."

Hayley looked over at Jarret, but he was fiddling with the radio and didn't look up.

Shasta's house was hard to find. It was almost hidden by shrubs and scrawny trees, and was set way off the road.

Jarret gunned the engine to start up the gravel driveway toward the tiny wooden house and stones sprayed out from behind his back wheels. "I'd hate to have to drive up here in the winter," he said. "It must be pure ice."

"Spooky," Ryan remarked.

Jarret pulled up at the front steps and a huge gray-and-white dog unfolded itself from the porch that ran along the front of the house. The dog stretched one leg, then the other, then yawned. Its tail thumped on the steps as it hobbled down to greet them.

"Do you think it'll bite?" Ryan asked, looking out at it.

"Ryan, the thing must be about a hundred years old. I don't think it has any teeth," Jarret said, laughing. "Look, he's smiling at you."

The ancient dog did seem to be grinning, its great black lips spread across its few remaining teeth. As Ryan stepped out, it gave one wobbly *woof*. Ryan dove back into the car, slamming the door.

Jarret laughed louder. "Don't be such a wimp, Ryan. C'mon, boy." He put his arm out through the open window and snapped his fingers. The dog sniffed at them, then gave them one long slow lick. "Look at him, he's a pussycat." Jarret studied the clouded eyes. "And he's blind, Ryan. I don't think he's much of a threat."

Still watching the dog, Ryan got out and went to the door. He looked around for a doorbell, shrugged, then knocked on the screen. The wood door behind it was open.

He stood waiting, his hands in his pockets. Hayley could

hear voices, Shasta's and another one – the second one
high and demanding – but she couldn't figure out what
they were saying. Finally Shasta opened the door and came
out. She followed Ryan down the steps, ran her fingers
along the ridge of the old dog's back, and got into the car.

"Hi, Shasta," Hayley said, as Shasta sat down behind
Jarret. "I like your skirt." It was short and denim, with
tiny leather fringes along the pockets. This was the first
time Hayley had seen Shasta wear anything but jeans.
Tonight she had a soft blue sweater tucked into the skirt.
Thin silver hoops were in her ears.

She smiled at Hayley. "Thanks," she said. She didn't
look at Ryan, just sat on the opposite side of the car from
him, her shoulder against the door and her fingers gripping the handle.

Ryan and Jarret talked all the way to the Video Cave,
discussing the latest football games and an upcoming
citywide basketball tournament. Whenever there was a
lull in the conversation, Hayley turned around and tried
to talk to Shasta, but the girl just nodded or shook her
head. Once, when Ryan was describing a football play to
Jarret, Hayley glanced at Shasta and saw her staring at
Ryan with such an open look in her eyes that Hayley
quickly turned back to face the front, feeling as though
she had somehow spied on her.

Jarret left the radio playing softly when he and Ryan
went into the Cave.

"I hope you don't mind, Shasta," Hayley said, sitting

sideways so she could face her. "We're just going back to Jarret's place. It should be okay, though."

"Sure," Shasta said.

Hayley cleared her throat, trying to think of something more to say. "Was that your grandmother talking when we were waiting for you?"

"Yeah. She always makes such a fuss about everything."

"Is it . . . just you two?"

Shasta nodded. "We moved here about two years ago." She looked out the window at a group of kids who were sitting on the hood of the car beside them. "Everything is so different here – the weather, the food, but especially the people. The people are really different."

Hayley wanted to ask her more. *What happened to your parents? Where did you live before? In what way are people different here?* But then Jarret and Ryan came back with the videos and those long plastic bags of yellow popcorn, and Hayley didn't say anything more to Shasta on the ride to Jarret's house.

They filed into the room off the living room. Jarret's mother called it the den and had made it cozy with lots of cushions piled on a big soft chair and two couches. Everything faced the wall unit that held the TV and VCR and CD player.

"What do you want to see first?" Jarret asked, squatting on his heels in front of the VCR. He waited, looking over his shoulder.

Hayley dropped onto one of the couches, looking at the two videos Ryan had tossed on the coffee table.

"I don't care." She leaned forward and picked one up. "Maybe this one." She held it up toward Shasta, who was standing uncertainly by the other couch. "*Camp Ivanhoe. It's supposed to be funny. And it's got to be better than that one.*" She gestured with her chin. "*Blood Trackers.* Ugh." The cover showed a girl with her mouth open in a silent scream, a looming figure reflected in her horrified eyes. "Some of those scary ones give me the creeps. Do you like them, Shasta?"

Shasta shook her head. Ryan perched on the arm of the couch Shasta was standing near and patted the seat. "Sit down, Shasta. Hey, Jarret, got anything to drink?"

"Yeah. Check the fridge." As Ryan left the den, Jarret held out his hand to Hayley. "Okay. Give me the camp one."

He slid the tape in, pressed PLAY, then sat down beside Hayley, putting his arm around her shoulders. Ryan came in swinging a six-pack of beer by its plastic collar.

"Hey, come on, man, don't drink my dad's beer," Jarret said, frowning. "He'll be on my case."

Ryan pulled one loose and popped the tab. "He won't miss a couple," he said, pulling another free and handing it to Shasta. Shasta looked at it, then at Ryan. She reached out and took it, glancing at Hayley. Hayley was staring at the television.

*

Partway into the movie Hayley heard Ryan whispering something. Then she heard Shasta laugh, really quietly. The laugh had an excited sound, but there was something else in it, too, something that bothered Hayley.

A few minutes later she heard it again, the whispering, then the laugh. It was the same kind of sound she remembered her younger sister making when she was small. She loved being tickled, but her squeals of laughter always carried the tiniest undercurrent of panic.

At that minute Ryan stood up. "This movie sucks. I don't feel like watching it."

"It's not that bad," Hayley said. "But it's taking a long time to get into it."

"Put on some music, Jarret," Ryan suggested, opening another beer. He tilted his head back and took a long swallow. "Want another one, Shasta?"

"No, thanks," she answered, putting the can to her mouth and taking a tiny sip. "I still have some."

Ryan walked to the wall unit and started flipping through the CDs. "Where's all the good stuff, Jarret? Who *are* all these people?"

"Those are my parents'. Mine are in my room." Jarret stood up. "I'll go get some. Hayley, you want a drink? Or some of that popcorn?"

"Yeah, I'll get a bowl." Hayley took the bag and went out to the kitchen. When she came back with two cans of soda and the popcorn in a big wooden salad bowl, music was pulsing from the CD player.

Ryan was standing in the middle of the room drinking his beer, his head moving slightly to the music, and Shasta, her legs curled under her, was looking up at him.

"Want some?" Hayley asked, shouting over the music, holding the popcorn bowl out to Shasta. Shasta took one piece. "Come on, take a handful." She saw Shasta looking at the soda. "Do you want one?"

Shasta's mouth moved, but Hayley had to lean closer to hear her. "What?"

"I said yes, please. I don't really like beer."

Hayley handed a can to her, walked around Ryan, and turned the volume down a notch. "Too loud, Ryan."

Ryan grabbed her by the waist. "Dance with me, Hayley."

Hayley swayed halfheartedly for a few seconds. "I don't like this stuff. Who is it?"

"Dunno. Something that was in the pile. Old folks' tunes. Where's Jarret, with his . . . oh, about time." He took the stack of CDs from him. "Here's a good one," he said, and put it on. The first song was soft and slow.

"C'mon, Jarret, let's dance," Hayley said, pushing the coffee table out of the way. Jarret put his arms around her and she put her cheek against his and they danced together, perfectly in time to the music.

Ryan held out his arms to Shasta, but she lowered her eyes and started winding a long strand of hair around her fingers. He bent down and pulled her up. Wrapping his arms around her and setting his chin on top of her head, he started to move back and forth. After a minute Shasta slowly raised her hands and put them on his back, her fingertips barely grazing his sweater.

When the song ended, Hayley opened her eyes and smiled up at Jarret. As the next song started, a faster one, she looked around. She could see Ryan and Shasta, still dancing, but they'd moved out into the living room.

"What do you think about those two?" she asked, taking a mouthful of her soda and gesturing to the living room. She handed the can to Jarret.

"Who knows?" he said. "Does she ever say anything?"

"She's just shy. Maybe she'll feel more comfortable if they're out there, away from us. Let's put that other movie on, okay? It might be better than the first one."

They started watching *Blood Trackers*. After a few minutes, Hayley glanced out to the living room. Ryan and Shasta were sitting on the couch in the semidarkness. Hayley turned to Jarret. "This movie doesn't look like it's going to be that bad, after all," she said. "I should tell Ryan and Shasta to come watch it."

"Leave them," Jarret said, his lips against her ear. "I like it better like this, just the two of us."

Hayley turned her face toward his. "Okay," she whispered, into his mouth.

The movie had a lot of loud music and roaring motor-cycles. Finally there was a quiet part. The girl and her boyfriend were hiding in an underground room. There

was no sound from the TV except for a few squeaks and
shuffling noises as the couple crept along the dirt floor.

Hayley lifted her head from Jarret's chest and brushed
her hair off her forehead. "Did you hear something?"

"Like what?"

"I don't know. I thought I heard something." She
looked toward the living room again. The couch was
empty. She strained to hear more, then got up. "I'm just
going to see where Shasta is."

"Leave them, Hayley."

"I just want to see. Be right back."

She went through the living room, poking her head
into the kitchen. It was deserted, too. She started softly
down the hall. Then, wondering why she was tiptoeing,
she strode along, heading toward the washroom. She saw
that the door to Jarret's bedroom was shut. She switched
on the bathroom light and closed the door, looking at
herself in the mirror over the sink. She ran her fingers
through her hair and took a drink of water. Then she
turned off the light and walked back down the hall.
When she got to Jarret's room, her footsteps slowed. She
stopped outside the closed door. There was a rustling
sound from inside, then a *thud*.

She took a step closer, holding her breath. She heard
an unintelligible, almost urgent whisper, and then
Shasta's voice – clear, loud – saying, "No, don't."

Hayley tensed, waiting. She heard another murmur, and
again the no. This time it had a pleading sound. "Please,

no. I don't want to." There was more rustling, the under-tones of Ryan's voice, Shasta's answer. "I said no. Stop it."

Hayley put her thumb to her mouth, biting at the nail. She looked down the hall toward the blue light of the TV in the den, then back at the closed door. She put her hand out, her fist clenched to knock, when there was a sudden louder sound. A rasping, choking noise. Hayley stepped back, pressing her fist against her mouth, listening to the panting ugly sound. She couldn't tell if it was Ryan or Shasta.

Hayley ran down the hall, through the living room, and back to the den. Jarret was on the couch where she'd left him, staring straight ahead, his hand in the popcorn bowl. "Jarret. Jarret," she said, kneeling beside him. "Ryan and Shasta are in your room."

Jarret didn't take his eyes off the screen. He snorted. "Typical. Trust Ryan. Just makes himself at home."

"Jarret." Hayley shook his arm and he looked at her.

"Hey, what's wrong? You look all –"

"I think Shasta's crying, Jarret. I'm sure I heard her crying or something."

"So?"

"She was saying no and, I don't know, maybe some-thing's happening, maybe Ryan . . ." Her voice trailed off. "Go see, okay, Jarret?"

Jarret stared at her. "Are you crazy? What am I gonna do? The bedroom police bit? Charge in and demand to know what they're up to? Leave them alone. She was

probably laughing. Probably having the time of her life."
He pulled her down beside him. "Come on, relax, Halo.
What they do isn't our business."

Hayley stayed perched on the edge of the couch,
trying not to think of the sounds she'd heard. She felt like
she had when she was a little girl watching TV with her
parents. Whenever there was something gruesome and
violent, her dad would make some lame joke and try to
put his hands over Hayley's eyes. If things got too bad, he
or her mother would take the remote and click to another
station. But tonight there were no jokes. There was no
way to change the channel.

Hayley put her hand on Jarret's arm. "Jarret," she
pleaded, looking at him. He didn't turn his head. "Jarret."
She shook his arm, her voice louder, more insistent.

Suddenly there was the sound of a door opening,
closing, opening again. Then, *slam*. Jarret dug into the
popcorn bowl. "Watch this part, Hayley. I think it's that
axe part they always show on the previews." His voice was
unnaturally loud. "Just watch."

Just like her dad. *Don't look, don't listen. If you can't see
or hear something ugly, it isn't happening.*

Hayley looked at the screen and saw the blood, the
open screaming mouth. Suddenly she felt sick. She
thought she was going to vomit.

"Jarret, please." Her fingers tightened their grip. Jarret
turned toward her, his eyes unreadable, his face reflecting
the violent colors from the screen. "Do something," she

begged. "Do something." Hayley didn't know what she wanted Jarret to do, didn't know why she couldn't get off the couch herself and run down the hall and stop what was happening, didn't know why she was waiting for Jarret. She reached across him with her free hand, grabbed the remote, and snapped off the movie. Everything stopped. There was no more sound. She let go of Jarret's arm. Her fingers were aching.

Ryan's voice, unexpected, made her jump. "Hey, Jarret, your dad got any more beer around anywhere? I'm parched. Oh, there's still part of one here."

Hayley looked to the doorway. Ryan's face was flushed, his carefully styled hair hanging over his forehead in stiff gelled strips. She watched him take Shasta's beer off the floor, put his lips to the opening, and finish it with a loud gurgling.

"Where's Shasta?" Hayley asked. "Where is she?"

"In the bathroom," he said, flopping into the chair. "Hey, what happened to the movie?"

Jarret clicked the VCR on with the remote, and Hayley leaned back and pretended to watch the movie. After a few minutes she realized Shasta was there. Out of the corner of her eye she could see her, a silhouette in the doorway. Hayley didn't have the nerve to turn her head and look at her.

Instead, she stood up. "I have to go," she said. She glanced toward the doorway, but she still couldn't see Shasta clearly.

"Hey, it's still early," Jarret said. "You never have to go home this early."

"I said I want to go, Jarret."

"Yeah," Ryan agreed, "let's split, get something to eat." He got up and walked toward Shasta.

Hayley waited for Jarret to turn out the lights and lock the house. By the time they came out to Jarret's car, Ryan and Shasta were already in the backseat.

Nobody said anything for a few blocks, then Ryan called out, "Hey, Jarret, stop for a burger."

"Sure. You hungry, Hayley?"

She shook her head. "Not really. I'd rather just go home."

"Come on, Hayley," Jarret said. "At least have a drink or something."

Again Ryan called from the back, "Yeah, Hayley. You girls can't go home on empty stomachs." Then he leaned over the front seat and put his mouth close to Jarret's head. "But make sure it's a take-out place." He ended the sentence with a low laugh.

Jarret joined him. "I hear you, man."

Hearing Jarret laugh with Ryan started a hard knot of anger in Hayley's throat. She wanted to take her hand, make a fist, and punch Jarret on the arm, on the leg, somewhere. She felt like punching. The knot was still there when Jarret pulled up to the drive-through window at the Night Owl. "What'll it be?" he asked, looking over at Hayley.

"Nothing." Hayley slouched in the seat, staring straight ahead.

"You sure?"

Hayley turned her head away.

"Order me a double burger, with the works, and a Giant Frosted," Ryan said.

Jarret turned around. "Shasta?"

Silence.

"Don't you want something, baby?" Ryan asked.

Order something, Shasta, Hayley thought. *Order lots of food, more than you can eat. Make Ryan pay.*

But when there was only silence, Jarret ordered what Ryan had asked for, with fries and a drink for himself, got the bags from the pickup window, and parked along the side of the lot. He and Ryan ate quickly, without talking, and as they were finishing, Ryan rolled down the window and called to someone in a car parked a few spots away.

"It's a couple of guys from the team. I think I'll catch up with them." He crumpled his hamburger wrapper and shoved it into the bag, then tossed the bag to Jarret. "Can you give Shasta a lift home, Jarret?"

Hayley turned around to see Ryan pick up Shasta's hand. She was huddled against the door, her face in darkness.

"You don't mind, Shasta," he told her. "I have some business to discuss with these guys before the practice tomorrow. Go over some plays, you know. Guy stuff." He said "guy stuff" in a silly singsong voice, making fun of himself. "It might take awhile." He put Shasta's hand down and kissed her cheek. "Had a great time, baby," he said. "Hey, Jarret, take her straight home. The old lady sounded like she could swing a mean punch." He laughed as he opened the car door, but it seemed forced.

Hayley watched him get out, still drinking his Giant Frosted, and she could see that Shasta was wiping at her cheek with her palm.

As they pulled out of the lot, Jarret turned on the radio, but the music didn't do anything to the hollowness in the car. No one said anything all the way to Shasta's house.

The front windows were brightly lit as they pulled up the driveway. Shasta jumped out the minute the car stopped. Hayley got out, too, finally daring to look at her.

It was a black autumn night, but Shasta was faintly illuminated by the lights from the house. Her face seemed to have melted, the features run together. Hayley saw that one of her earrings was missing. "Are you all right, Shasta?" she asked softly.

Shasta picked at the fringes of her skirt pocket.

Hayley dug in her bag for her brush. "Your grandma will kill you if you go in looking like this." Shasta looked at the brush without taking it. Hayley put it back in her purse and pulled out a tissue. She reached out and touched one of the black smudges under Shasta's eyes. "Your mascara."

Shasta took the tissue, balling it up in her hand. "It doesn't matter," she said, walking away.

Hayley watched Shasta's back, fighting down the sick feeling she'd had since Jarret's house. "Bye," she called, louder than necessary.

Shasta's hand raised in a wave.

"Shasta?" The girl stopped. "Ryan's a jerk, Shasta. He's always been a jerk."

Shasta walked up the porch stairs. The dog lifted its massive head and sniffed the air, gray ears cocked. Hayley saw her bend down and rub the dog behind its ears. From that distance she looked tiny.

Hayley didn't want to leave yet. She called out, "Hey Shasta. Want to come over tomorrow? To my house?" Shasta straightened her back, her head still lowered over the dog. "Maybe you can show me how to do that braid; the one you wore to school once. It looked really neat." Hayley's voice sounded artificial, even to her own ears.

Shasta finally raised her eyes and looked straight into Hayley's. She walked back down the steps, stopping on the bottom one. "No. I'm cutting my hair, anyway."

They stared at each other for a moment.

"Hayley?" Shasta's voice was so quiet that Hayley had to move away from the car, so she could hear her better.

"Yeah? What? What, Shasta?" It was still there, that false eager tone. Hayley realized that she wanted Shasta to say it didn't matter, she understood that Hayley couldn't have done anything or changed what happened. Hayley wanted Shasta to take away the horrible suffocating feeling she had. The feeling that something had happened to her, too, not just to Shasta.

"Why didn't you warn me?" Shasta asked. "If you knew he was such a jerk, you could have told me." That was all she said. Those two sentences. Then she turned and walked back up the steps.

Hayley went to the car and got in. "Go," she told Jarret.

"She okay?" he asked. When Hayley didn't answer, he started to back down the long gravel driveway. There was no place to turn around. "Hey, Halo." He cleared his throat. "There's a practice tomorrow afternoon."

"Don't call me Halo anymore, okay?"

Jarret shrugged. He watched the rearview mirror and continued to back up slowly. "So I'll pick you up at one, for the practice."

"No."

They had reached the end of the driveway. Jarret eased to a stop, looked at her. "No? Why not?"

"I hate watching football practice."

"You hate it? Since when? You always said you loved coming."

"Well, I don't. Since always." Hayley's words were rushed. "I only said I loved it because I knew you liked me to watch you. But I never really wanted to come." She rubbed the back of her hand across her mouth, wiping off what was left of her lipstick. "And I'm not coming anymore."

She looked toward Shasta's house and Jarret followed her eyes. They could see Shasta, illuminated by the headlights from the car. She was sitting beside the dog, her arms around its neck, her face buried in the curling hair of its back.

Jarret gave one *toot* on the horn, but Shasta didn't lift her head. He waited a moment, then honked again.

He kept on. Short loud honks, over and over, until Hayley reached out and put her hand on his arm, stopping him, stopping the noise.

Starlight, Star Bright

*P*lease *don't be late this time. Please don't be late.*

Holding the living-room curtain aside, Jessie squeezed her eyes shut. She visualized the candy-apple red Corvette slowly rumbling up the snowy street and coming to rest in front of the house, with its engine idling and Dean giving his usual two honks on the horn. The power of positive thinking.

Jessie opened her eyes. The street was still; no tire tracks marked the fresh layer of white.

Please don't be any later. Jessie's lips moved in a steady rhythm, turning the phrase into a silent incantation.

"So you're waiting for him again, eh? When do you think His Lordship will show up this time? Or will he make it at all?" Jessie turned from the window. Her mother was leaning against the peeling kitchen door frame, watching her. Her chapped red hands were jammed into the pockets of the apron that was tied loosely around her cashier's smock.

Just come, Dean. I don't care how late you are. Just come.

"Wishing on a star won't do any good, you know, Jessie."

"He'll be here, Mom. We're going to a movie." Jessie glanced at the big wet flakes of snow starting to build into tiny drifts along the curb. "Dean had to drive one of his friends to a basketball game first, way over in the west end," she said, watching the reflection of her eyes in the window, the lie coming out of nowhere. "But he'll be here. I know he will." She licked her lips, pushed her blonde hair behind her ears.

Her mother shook her head just the tiniest bit. "*Mmmm.*"

She pretends she hasn't heard about it – Dean and that snobby girl from the Heights last year. I know she knows, and that's why she doesn't like him, but she won't come out and say it. She doesn't know Dean like I do. He told me what really happened, the whole story.

Her mother sighed as she slowly lowered herself onto the sagging couch. "I don't know why you have to set your sights on the highest tree in the forest, Jessie." She took off her white rubber-soled shoes and set her feet on the coffee table. "Boys who look like Dean, boys who drive fancy little cars and live over in the Heights, don't take out girls from around here."

Jessie didn't turn around. "Of course they do, Mother." She stressed the Mother. "That's a ridiculous thing to say."

"Yeah? Who else do you know dating a boy like Dean? I tell you, Jessie, I don't like it." She reached forward and prodded the instep of one foot with her thumbs, sighing softly.

"You've never liked any of the boys I've gone out with."

"I liked that short one – what was his name? – Michael. Your brother's friend from the apartments in the next block. Now he was a nice kid."

"Yeah. A nice kid. That's all he was. He was never a real boyfriend. He was Kenny's friend, that's all, and some-times I just went along with them wherever they were going."

"And why do you think he hung around with your brother? To get closer to you. There are lots of boys around here who would give anything to go out with you, Jessie." She groaned as she swung her feet down. "You could have your pick."

Jessie pulled at a tiny thread in the dull brocade of the curtain.

Her mother tried to push one foot into her shoe. "It was just the other day, come to think of it, that I heard something about that Michael from Irene, the one who works in Produce. She said Michael was an altar boy when he was younger." She frowned and kicked both shoes to one side. "Yeah. There was something special about him. I liked him."

Jessie turned around, letting the curtain close. "Well, that's nice, Mother. Like him all you want. I liked him too, but as a friend." She sat down on the arm of the chair in front of the window, then half turned so she could pull the curtain aside. She fixed her eyes on the street again. "Yeah, he was okay. But I'm serious about Dean, Mom, really serious. Being in love with someone and being friends, just buddies, are two entirely different things."

Her mother snorted. "Oh, so now you're in love." She dragged out the word, making it sound like *luuv*.

Jessie sat up straighter on the chair's arm, lowered her eyelids, and stared at her mother from under them. "See? Why do I even bother? You never try to understand. Yes, Mom, it just so happens I'm in love. I love Dean. So what are you going to do about it?" She opened her eyes wider, trying to look bold, unafraid.

Her mother sat perfectly still. "And does he love you, too, Jess? Does he tell you that? Tells you he loves you when you're all cuddled up in that red car?"

Jessie's eyes dropped to the worn carpet. She scraped the toe of her sneaker back and forth across the faded pattern. "I know he loves me," she said. She kept looking at the carpet.

Her mother's voice was softer than usual. "I do know what you're talking about, Jessie. I've seen you with Dean, seen the way you look at him, how you . . ." She stopped, then started again. "A lot of those feelings, the ones you call love, are the feelings you have when you first meet someone. That excitement . . ." She stopped again, and Jessie could almost hear her thinking. Jessie kept her eyes fixed on her sneaker as it swung back and forth, back and forth.

Her mother cleared her throat. "Well, you know what I mean. The . . . the physical side," she said. Jessie looked up to see her mother gazing at the coffee table, then leaning forward and picking at a small dry piece of something stuck on the dull wood. She scratched at it with her fingernail. "Those feelings don't last forever, girl."

Jessie watched her mother's busy scraping. *Those feelings. She can't even say the word. Sometimes I wonder if she's ever felt it.*

Her mother got off whatever was on the table, but she started rubbing at the spot with her fingers, as if she were trying to bring back some shine to the wood. She left the table alone for a moment and ran her hand through her short graying hair. Then she started rubbing again, squinting down at the table. "No, it doesn't last all that long. But friendship . . . well, strong dependable friendship is really what love is about, Jessie." Her fingers slowed, then rubbed harder, up and down, across, polishing. "Like the moon. At times full and bright and glowing, other times dim, and sometimes hidden. Always changing, but always there."

Jessie stared at her mother's fingers, at their busy rhythmic motion.

"No, it's not the stars that are so beautiful and wondrous. They explode or collapse and fall away and you never see them again. But if you're very lucky, you find that the moon and the stars can work together. When one star burns itself out, the light from the moon will get you through until you see the next star."

Jessie slid from the arm of the chair down into the seat. She couldn't stop watching the hypnotic movements of her mother's fingers, afraid if she stopped watching her mother would stop talking. Her mother had never said this much at one time.

"You know, Jessie, I think the stars are the treats life sometimes lets you have, the little pockets of joy. But they're not what life and love are about. They're not the whole thing."

Her mother stopped rubbing, and there was silence in the room. Jessie raised her eyes and looked at her mother's face.

"No, Jess. The stars aren't everything."

Jessie sat forward, her mouth partly open, willing her mother to go on.

"Now, take your dad."

Jessie slumped back, twitched her shoulders. The mention of her dad had spoiled it all. For just a few moments she had thought that maybe her mom was really onto something. She'd never heard her talk like that, as if she were dreaming out loud. As if she weren't a cashier down at ByLine's. As if she didn't let herself get pushed around.

"I knew your dad from the time we were kids out in the country. He was my friend; I liked him a long time before there was any of the other business."

There she goes again. That "other business." She doesn't know anything about my relationship with Dean, but she thinks sex must be all he's interested in. And she doesn't give me much credit for making up my own mind. I made it really clear to Dean, just last week, that I wouldn't go any further. He got pretty mad, but I know it'll be all right once he knows I mean it.

"And you know something, Jessie? That good friendly feeling has stayed through thick and thin – like they say, for better or for worse."

Same old story. I've heard it a hundred times. Jessie started chewing at her bottom lip, but stayed quiet while her mother continued.

"Yeah. Even through all your dad's layoffs and troubles at work, even when we've been flat broke, we've always –"

"Sometimes you just make me sick, Mom, talking about Dad and your devotion to each other." Jessie put her hands on the arms of the chair and stood up. "Do you know how many times I've heard you tell me what a good man Dad is? It's all a bunch of garbage." Her hands stayed on the arms of the chair, her knuckles turning white. "What about all the times you've had to work double shifts, Mom, dead on your feet, and then come home to a black eye or split lip? And the times when Dad hasn't bothered to show up for days at a time? What about the times he's spent his whole paycheck on booze, or given it away to the complete stranger who was his best buddy for the hour Dad was buying? What's shining then, Mom? The moon or the stars?"

Jessie's chest heaved as she finished. The words had been so strong, so sure, but in the silence that followed, staring into her mother's eyes, she suddenly released her hands, dropping into the soft hollow of the chair's seat with a dull *thud*.

Her mother finally blinked, fast, then faster, and Jessie saw the skin around her mouth sag in an unfamiliar way. She got up quickly, grabbing her white shoes and walking to the kitchen.

Jessie stayed in the chair listening, and in a moment heard water running and the clinking of dishes. *Mom's other solace, besides her rosary.*

Jessie could picture her mother standing at the deep, stained sink with her hands immersed in the hot soapy water. She had often come into the kitchen and noticed the calm in her mother's face as she pressed against the worn counter, fingering the chipped plates and heavy mugs and mismatched spoons and knives and forks in the murky warmth.

Jessie's lips curved downward. *Imagine having so little comfort in life that washing dishes is a pleasure. I'll never be like her. Never.*

She sat in the shadowed living room, trying not to think about the way her mother had looked when Jessie had said her piece about her dad. Then she heard the water gurgling out of the sink, and the shuffle of her mother's stocking feet down the hall.

On the wall behind the couch, under the crucifix, was the clock Jessie and Kenny had given their mother for Christmas. The brass rays around the face of the clock made it look like a sun. Her mother had wanted that clock for a long time.

Tonight the clock seemed to be ticking louder than usual, calling Jessie to look. She refused at first, getting up on her knees to pull the curtain back from the window and tuck it behind the chair so she had a clear view of the street. But the ticking just kept on. *Jes-sie. Jes-sie.*

When she finally looked over her shoulder at it, she saw how late it was. The show would have started, would be well into the second half. *Too late to go now.*

The room grew colder. Jessie ran her fingers up and down the wood around the window, feeling the tiny finger of freezing air snaking in around the crumbling caulking. She shivered suddenly, and rubbed her upper arms with her hands as she went down the dark narrow corridor to her bedroom. Grabbing her heavy sweater from the end of her bed and sliding it over her head, she passed her parents' bedroom. A loud creak made her stop and look through the doorway. The moonlight flooding in through the window showed her father's bulky form shifting under a pile of blankets and settling on his back. As she watched, he started snoring, a rough grating noise.

Then she saw her mother on the far side of the room, sitting on the little wooden chair near the closet, her head down. Jessie could see the glint of the rosary beads that were wound around her hands. She stood there, looking at her mother, hearing the growling harshness of her father's snoring. All of a sudden two familiar beeps sounded, two small dull beeps.

Jessie's mother raised her head and looked at Jessie in the doorway.

Even when the honks sounded again, Jessie didn't move. Her father's snoring kept on, getting louder, growing with the same persistence as the car horn.

Jessie backed away and walked into the living room, glancing at the clock. After eleven-thirty. Too late to go anywhere but the parking spot Dean liked to go to at the end of an evening. *Or anytime.*

She watched the clock as she slowly sat down on the couch where her mother had been sitting earlier. She put her hands between her knees, pressing them together until the seams of her jeans started to dig into the skin on the back of her hands, hurting. When she heard a muffled spinning of tires, she went to the door and looked out through the diamond of glass in the heavy wood.

The Corvette had already wheeled around on the street. Jessie watched until the swaying red taillights turned the corner. She snapped off the porch light and tilted her head sideways so she could look up. The snow had stopped, and the sky was black and empty except for the round white moon.

She pulled off her sweater and walked down the hall again, this time closing her bedroom door behind her with a quiet *click*.

Show Time

*T*wo things happened during the hottest summer on record in our town. I got my first period and I met Little Leon.

There are two main events in town each year – the winter carnival and the summer fair. These happenings are typical for small towns in Manitoba; maybe for small towns everywhere.

The fair always lasts four days, with all the expected local activities. There are craft sales and homemade goodies to buy, everything from apple jelly to zucchini chutney. Then there's a full day of livestock judging, with all the hopeful 4-H kids standing around in the suffocating heat and stench of the animal tent, brushing their calves and trying to get their spring pigs to stop rooting long enough for the judge to look them over.

Rides are rented from an outfit in Winnipeg that comes out and sets up the Ferris wheel and the Egg

Beater and the Moto Roto, as well as all the little kiddie cars and boats and ladybug rides. But the group from the States is what makes the fair an event. Every year they hit a whole bunch of places close to the border, spending two or three days at each town. When I was younger, I was really impressed by them, but last year they suddenly lost their appeal. I started to notice things I never had before – the potbellies and sweat-stained shirts of the older men as they spun their gambling wheels and the bored expressions of the younger guys, the ones with muscles and tattoos, as they tried, between sips of beer, to lure customers to their games. It seemed that even the stuffed raccoons and leopards and bears had a dusty despairing look as they swayed in the greasy clouds that rose from the miniature doughnut stand and the Lean Mean Hot Dog Machine.

The only thing that's still vaguely entertaining is the sideshow. It's always set up in a huge tattered tent out behind the midway, at the edge of old Hank Lindquist's field. Hank hasn't worked that field for years, but every summer he swaths about an acre of the wild grass so the show people can park their trailers there. For his trouble he and his ancient mother are given unlimited free passes for the rides and the sideshow. The sideshow charges a lot to get in – four dollars a head, even for kids – but it goes on for most of an hour and there's a lot to see.

The animal oddities are pretty typical – a downcast little donkey with a fifth leg hanging limply out of its hip, or a cow with two udders – but the animals themselves are never the same from year to year. Life on the road must not agree with them.

The human performances don't change as often. Each year I've watched Stella the Snake Girl roll around in a huge aquarium filled with a slithery hissing mass and Silver Tongue Sam swallow swords and run back and forth over a bed of nails without drawing blood.

Little Leon and Big Mama are regulars, too, but their act is different than the others'. Leon and Mama don't really do anything, yet they seem to get the loudest response. Leon's a tiny person, smaller than a five-year-old, and Mama is a huge sweating woman in a shapeless dress. She pushes an old carriage out onto the stage, then takes Little Leon out and sets him in a high chair. He always wears a fuzzy sleeper and a white frilly bonnet. After Mama leaves the stage on the pretense of getting a bottle, Leon puts a finger to his lips, warning the audience not to tell on him, then climbs out of the high chair and starts running around the stage, doing goofy baby somersaults and showing off. When Mama calls out, "Little Leon, are you being a good boy for Mama?" Leon sticks out his tongue at the curtain. Of course, at that moment, Mama comes out. She chases him around the stage, eventually pulling off his bonnet, and the crowd gasps when curly gray hair falls down around his shoulders. Then he rips open the top of his sleeper and sticks out his chest, which is covered with thick hair. The chase goes on for a few minutes longer, until Mama trips and falls, thrashing and squealing, her dress pulled up to expose huge bloomer-clad thighs with Little Leon trapped between them. The two eventually chase each other off the stage, down through the crowd, and disappear through the back flap of the tent with everyone clapping and roaring. It's more like a circus act than anything else, like one of those silly clown routines, but it's always at the end of the show and everyone leaves the tent laughing, ready for more rides and food.

Most Manitoba summers are hot, but this one had been such an unbelievable scorcher that for three whole weeks my mom kept our windows tightly closed and the blinds down. She claimed that the stifling hot winds could carry new strains of disease from as far away as Mexico. She said she once read about a similar situation in France, where some airborne African epidemic wiped out a whole village in Provence. My mom gets a lot of her information from old and unreliable sources, or else she shamelessly twists facts.

She says it was the extreme heat that finally brought on my period. The fact that I'm almost fifteen had nothing to do with it, according to her. She's convinced that without the heat, I might never have made it into the mysterious world of womanhood. When I told her that she could stop worrying, that it had finally happened, she smiled smugly and pulled out a tattered *National*

Geographic. She opened it to a series of pages showing bare-breasted, dark-skinned girls. Some held tiny babies on their hips as they stared into the camera, while others bent over gourds, pounding on something grainy while their toddlers slept strapped to their backs.

Mom tapped the glossy pages with a stubby index finger. "These girls are mothers and they're no more than twelve or thirteen, Angel," she said, pushing the magazine at me. "They must have got the curse real young. It's the heat, you see, the constant high temperatures. Brings the blood to maturation quicker than the cold." She lifted her glasses off the bridge of her nose and swiped at her face with the bottom of her apron. She always wears an apron at home, even though she doesn't do much cooking or cleaning.

"What about Maxine Warner?" I argued. "She got her period back in grade five during a blizzard."

Mom rearranged her glasses on her face and slammed the magazine shut, sending a puff of warm stale air into my face. "Those Warners, always showing off. You can't judge anything by Maxine. She's . . . well, between you and me, I don't think that girl has what it takes."

"Takes for what?"

"Just takes, that's all. No character. She's not like you, Angel. No, thank goodness. You girls are as different as night and day."

I didn't bother to point out that it was Maxine Warner and not me who got invited to all the parties. Maxine

Warner was not the oddball; I was the only one in my class who still had a flat chest and hips as straight as an eight-year-old boy's. But there's no point in arguing with someone who still refers to menstruation as the curse, or gives the name Angel to her only child.

In a small town everyone knows, right down to the day if not the moment, when you get your first bra or your first kiss. And Mom was one of the biggest Nosy Parkers. I've told her, more than a few times, that she shouldn't be so interested in everyone else's business, but she always says that after a lifetime of anonymous living in Montreal, she likes taking an active part in a real place. For my part, I've always thought that the real world, the one Mom and Dad were so eager to give up when I was only three, was just waiting for me to rejoin it.

"The Buxton girl is in the way, you know," Mom told me as she sat on my bed, watching me try to do something with my bush of red hair. After her Women of the Independent Oddfellows meeting that afternoon – she's president of the Rebekah Chapter – she was all up-to-date on local news.

"In the way of what?" I asked, wincing as the elastic I was winding around my thick ponytail snapped.

"In *the* way, of course. You know."

I put my arms down, shaking my hair around my face. "Pregnant, you mean?"

Mom frowned and nodded, her lips a straight line.

"So? Why can't you just come out and say the word? And anyway, big deal. She *is* married." I tried not to sigh, waiting for what I knew was coming next.

"*Mm-hmm.*" Mom's lips were so tight they disappeared altogether. "And exactly when did she get married? Only two months ago. A June bride. Big white wedding and all. And she's showing already. She's got to be at least four months along, maybe more." She fanned herself with the newsletter, closing her eyes.

I concentrated on my hair, not wanting to encourage her. Hard to believe this was a woman who once had an important job in a lab. I think maybe all those years glued to a microscope gave her a slightly cockeyed view of the world.

"What are you getting fixed up for?" she asked.

"I'm not getting fixed up," I said, giving up on the ponytail and trying a moss green hairband. "I'm just trying to do something with this hair. I hate it. If it was straighter, at least I could do a few things with it."

"It's lovely like that, back off your face. It makes you look so young and innocent."

I immediately pulled the hairband off, tossing it onto the dresser. Young and innocent was not the image I had in mind.

"Like the little girl I used to know." She sighed. "And now you're grown up. Do you feel any different, Angel?" She fingered the pages of her newsletter.

I looked at myself in the mirror on the back of my dresser. "Different?"

"Because of what happened the other day. Starting."

I picked up a pair of tweezers and pulled out one hair from my right eyebrow. "No. I feel exactly the same, except less comfortable. Nothing's changed."

I could see Mom reflected in the mirror. She had a little smile on her lips. "Everything's changed, Angel. You've crossed that line." She smoothed her apron over her lap. "Things are clearer on the other side of the line."

I watched her face. "What kind of things?"

"They're different for everyone. You'll know." She gave me a big smile, and suddenly looked years younger than half a century. "Now, why don't you go down to the fair?"

I started shuffling through the top drawer of my dresser, just moving stuff around. "I don't feel like going."

"Why ever not?" I shrugged, but Mom wouldn't let it drop. "A hot Saturday night in August and the fair in town? All the young people go." She put her hand into her apron pocket. "I know the allowance you get doesn't go far, Angel, so I want you to take this."

I looked at the crumpled twenty-dollar bill in her hand. "No, Mom. It's not the money. I just . . . don't feel like going."

Her freckled hand pushed it into mine. "You go on. Have a good time, buy some ice cream, and go on a ride or two. You've spent too much time out on the swing in the backyard this summer. It's good to be alone and daydream sometimes – lots of big ideas come from dreams born on swings – but still, Angel . . ."

I looked into her faded blue eyes, saw the concerned wrinkle between them, and suddenly, to my horror, felt the beginning of tears prickling at the back of my eyeballs. I shoved the bill into the pocket of my shorts and turned away, flipping my hair up and rubbing the damp skin on the back of my neck.

"Okay. Thanks. See you later." I didn't want to turn around, didn't want her to see my eyes, so I just left her sitting on my bed and started through the dark airless living room.

She called after me. "Tell your father to slip home for a decent bite of supper when he can. He volunteered to help Mr. Rossburn take tickets somewhere. I don't want him eating anything from those stands. Who knows how long that food sits in the hot sun?"

"All right," I yelled, and as the screen door slammed behind me, I could still hear her voice, warning me not to go on any rides that shook the spine. Something about popping vertebrae.

As I walked down the uneven sidewalk, which was made up of concrete squares divided by long springy tufts of quack grass, I counted the money from my pocket: the twenty from Mom and a few more dollars in quarters and dimes. Maybe I wouldn't go to the fair after all. I could just slip into the Milano Café, order a chocolate milkshake, and sit there in the air-conditioned coolness until enough time had passed that I could go home again.

I saw Loreen Dunn up ahead on the sidewalk, walking so slowly that it was impossible not to catch up to her. Loreen was in the grade ahead of me, and was one of the most popular girls in school. When I was a few steps behind her, she stopped and turned, her long blonde hair bouncing away from her shoulders in a perfect arc. Her hazel eyes looked surprised, or maybe just disappointed. She put her hands on her hips, arching her back slightly so that her breasts strained against the thin turquoise cotton of her tank top.

"Oh, it's you."

There didn't seem to be any appropriate reply. "Are you going to the fair?" I asked, mainly for something to say.

Loreen's eyebrows raised ever so slightly. "Of *course*, Angel. Where else would I be going?"

I brushed at a tuft of grass with the toe of my sandal. "Me, too. Meeting Rod?" *Was there no end to the idiotic questions that tumbled out of my mouth?* Loreen and Rod had been going out since Christmas.

Loreen started walking again, but this time her tanned legs took such long steps that I almost had to jog to keep up. She glanced at me. "We're double-dating. With Crystal and Rick."

I nodded, my heart giving this big painful kick against my chest. It happened whenever I heard Rick's name, or caught a glimpse of him in the hall at school, or even when I saw his dad's old pickup parked outside the hotel. Sometimes I walked by the truck and nonchalantly ran my hand over the passenger door handle, in case Rick had been the last one to touch it.

I never even got near to him. He was one of the guys who, every morning before classes, lined up on either side of the hallway leading to the girls' washroom. Running the gauntlet, the girls called it. Lots of them, including Loreen, made a big deal out of it, sauntering along in groups of twos or threes, pretending to be totally engrossed in their conversation. But the whole time their eyes flicked left and right, their hips swaying and their backs abnormally straight.

"If you can flaunt it, run the gauntlet" was the expression I made up for the silly game: the preening strut of the girls, the growling and yipping and exaggerated tongue-hanging of the boys. Those of us with nothing to flaunt refused to go near the washroom before first bell, calling the whole thing a ridiculous display. But maybe it was the fear of the imagined pall that would descend on the hallway if we hurried through, our shoulders rounded over the books clutched against unenviable chests.

As Loreen slowed down at the T where Walnut Avenue hit Main Street, I was finally able to match my stride with hers. Stopping, she peered at the far end of the street, past the hotel and the credit union, toward the tinny music and muffled shrieks from the fairgrounds. "Aren't you meeting someone? You're not going to the fair *alone*, are you?"

I kicked at a piece of loose shale on the edge of the sidewalk and squinted toward the opposite end of town, staring at the empty gravel road shimmering in the still heat of early evening. "Robyn and Merrie should be along any minute," I said, shading my eyes with my hand. It might be true. I had heard Robyn and Merrie talking about the fair this afternoon in Al's, and they would have to come down Main Street to get to the fair.

Loreen didn't even try to hide the relief on her face. She showed her teeth in a brief smile. The danger of having to walk any farther with me was past. "Great," she said, then left me standing at the corner. I watched her go, noticing that her swinging hair was almost the exact same honey color as her bare shoulders.

I tried staying in the café as long as I could, but got bored after about an hour. I came out and stood on the dead street. The music from the fair was loud, the air was cooling off, and I could smell something – a familiar smell, a tempting mixture of popcorn and cotton candy. It reminded me of when I was little and how excited I used to get about the fair. I had a sudden unexpected urge to go again.

At the fairgrounds I wandered around for a while, looking for Dad to tell him about supper. I finally found him reading outside the sideshow tent. He was sitting on a webbed lawn chair beside the closed flap and I had to say "Dad" three times before he looked up.

"Oh, hello, sweetheart," he said, closing the *New England Journal of Medicine* and glancing at his watch. "Are you here for the next show? It doesn't start for a while yet."

"No. Mom just wanted me to tell you to come home for something to eat when you're done."

He dismissed the message with a wave of his hand. "But you'll come to the show, won't you? It's your favorite part of the fair."

"Not tonight, Dad. Maybe I'll come tomorrow instead."

Dad took off his floppy straw hat and carefully wiped his glistening bald spot with a large plaid handkerchief. "This is your last chance, Angelfish." He blotted at the inside band of the hat. "The rides and concessions will stay up until tomorrow night, but the folks here want to pack up early and head out tomorrow morning." He settled the hat back on his head and picked up his journal. "Final show at 9:30. Tonight's your last chance," he repeated, his voice fading as he started to read again.

I bought a corn dog and stood eating it at the booth. Hearing a blast of laughter, I looked around. Loreen and Rod, Crystal and Rick were standing at the next booth, a water pistol game. Rod was swinging his prize, which was a green bamboo cane with an inflated banana dangling from the end, down the front of Loreen's tank top. Turning slightly so I could watch them out of the corner of my eye, I saw Loreen push away the banana and say something to Rick, glancing in my direction. Rick shook his head and crossed his arms over his chest, but then Crystal stood on her toes and whispered something to him. His face got this funny look, then he gave a little laugh and looked at me. I carefully examined my corn dog, as if there might be something live in the mealy batter, and when I took another peek in their direction I saw that Crystal had both arms twined around Rick's neck. I started to walk away, tossing my corn dog into a garbage bin.

"Angel. Hey, Angel, come here for a sec." It was Rick's voice. I'd never heard him say my name before, and suddenly it took on a magical sound. I turned, attempting indifference.

Rick motioned for me to come over. Crystal had stepped back beside Loreen and Rod. I walked toward them, aware that one leg of my shorts was riding up and the armpits of my T-shirt felt damp.

Rick looked back at the others. I looked, too. Their faces all had the same pleasant, vague expression. "We were wondering, Angel," he said, then stopped and scratched at a tiny bump just under his bottom lip. "We were all wondering, since your old man . . . your dad's taking tickets for the sideshow, if you could, you know, get us in. For free."

I'd never been this close to Rick before. I saw that there were tiny flecks of gold in the dark brown of his irises. His eyelashes looked as if he'd curled them with one of those metal torture-chamber tools they sell in the drugstore. The thudding of my heart seemed to be making it hard for me to hear properly.

"So? Can you get us in?" It was Crystal. "We're broke. The guys spent all their money trying to win the monster zebra for us."

I looked back to Rick.

"Whaddya say, Angel?" His voice was low, and as he spoke, his eyelids flickered, just once. I felt the flicker up my backbone.

"Sure. No problem." My own voice sounded unnaturally loud. In the split second of silence that followed, my mind was racing for a way to get around my dad. He was incredibly honest. He'd never dream of letting even *me* in without paying, let alone anyone else. I wiped my sweaty palms on my shorts and heard the tiny rustle of the bill in my pocket. Suddenly it was simple. I'd do anything to be around Rick.

"Wait here for a couple of minutes," I said. "I'll go straighten it out with my dad."

Rick reached out and squeezed my wrist. "Good girl," he said, not realizing the heat from his hand was burning right through my skin, turning the bone to a hot soupy mess. When he let go, my arm just dropped limply to my side, heavy but weightless at the same time.

"Be right back." The paralysis had traveled up my arm to my throat, and now my voice came out in a mousy squeak. I left the group at a stroll, but ended up sprinting the last few yards to the sideshow tent. There was still a good half hour until show time, but a long lineup had already formed. I had to wait an eternity before I got to the front.

I pulled out the twenty. "Hi, Dad. I'm coming after all, with four of my friends. I'll pay for us all now."

Dad took the bill and turned it over. "You treating?"

I studied a water stain on the tent, just over his shoulder. "We all chipped in. Can you hurry, Dad?" I held out my hand.

He unrolled five purple stubs and ripped them off slowly, with the tiny tremor all his movements had now.

I took the end of the tickets. "Thanks. I'll be right back." I looked behind me and saw Rick and the others slowly walking in the direction of the tent. I gave a little tug on the tickets, but Dad was still holding on to them. I turned back to him. Dad's eyes were on Rod and Loreen, Crystal and Rick.

"Are those your friends, Angel?"

I shrugged. "Yeah. Sort of. I gotta go, Dad."

"Could you do something for me first?"

"Dad." I threw another glance over my shoulder. The four of them had stopped by the Ferris wheel.

"It's Little Leon. You know, from the show," Dad said. "He gave me a prescription to fill this morning and I said I'd bring it down to him." He held out a small white bag that was stapled at the top. "It's all paid for. His trailer is the one with a dog's head on the door. Just knock and hand it in to him." He looked at me. "It's important,

Angel. And I can't leave here until the show is under way."
He let go of the tickets.

I stared at the bag, then grabbed it, shoving the tickets
in my pocket. As I started to push through the flap of the
tent, I looked back at the Ferris wheel and held up my
hand, five fingers spread. "Five minutes," I mouthed.
Rick answered with a kind of salute.

I made my way through the hazy dimness of the half-
full tent and left through the back flap. Behind the huge
tent the atmosphere was hushed, the humming noise of
the fair distorted. In the rough empty field that stretched
to nowhere, the row of dilapidated tin trailers sat like
squat orange-tinged bugs, reflecting the last low streaks
of the sun.

I walked past the first trailer, glancing inside. A thin
man with a mustache like a black line was lying on a cot,
his arm thrown over his eyes and his bare feet hanging
over the end of the bed. A tiny white kitten stretched out
on his chest. Outside the next trailer a woman wearing a
gold sequin-covered bathing suit sat on a folding wooden
chair. She was bent over her black fishnet stockings with
a needle and thread. As I passed, she looked up. Black
eyeliner was caked in the creases around her eyes, and her
heavy makeup didn't cover all the old pits and scars
dotting her cheeks.

"Hi, kid. Whaddya doin' back here?"

I held the bag straight out in front of me. "I'm taking
this to Little Leon. It's okay. I mean, my dad sent me with

this. He's the pharmacist. I'm supposed to be here." I was talking so fast I was almost babbling. I felt as if I were somehow trespassing, as if I might see something I didn't want to see.

The woman grinned. "You better watch out, girlie. Mama don't like anyone messing with her baby." She lowered her head and snipped at the thread with her front teeth, then looked up at me and gave one short howl. "Just kiddin'. Jeez, don't look so scared."

I attempted the look Loreen had given me earlier, wanting to blow the woman off with a worldly annoyed expression, but her head was bent again, examining the thick twisted line of stitching on her thigh.

The next two trailer doors were closed. The fifth one had a small silhouette of a dog's head nailed to it. I stepped up on the wooden crate in front of the door and knocked. A low-pitched voice answered my knock. "Yes?"

Putting my head around the opening, I saw Little Leon sitting on a big cushion on a bench pulled up to a card table. He wasn't dressed in his baby outfit, but wore a crisp blue-and-white striped shirt and a pair of jeans. His hair was tied back in a neat ponytail and he looked like a regular middle-aged man, except for his size. There was an empty glass on the table in front of him.

"Come on in," he said, his face tired but friendly. "Do you want to take a picture?"

"No, my dad asked me to give you this." I stepped through the doorway to hand him the bag, but stopped.

I don't know why. I just felt funny going up to him, towering over him, even though I'm shorter than anyone else my age.

Leon looked at the bag and smiled. "You're Frank's daughter?"

"Yes. Angel. My name's Angel."

"Ah, Angel. What a beautiful name," Leon said. "Your parents must have had such confidence in you to give you a name that would require a great deal of character to live up to."

I stood there, still holding the bag. "I don't know about that. I've never liked it."

"A name is important," Leon said, his voice deep and calm. "I wasn't always called Leon." He pronounced it Lay-on. "I chose it for myself, when I was old enough to realize my situation. The name Leon always filled me with inspiration and pride. It has a certain air of grandeur, don't you think?"

I nodded, licking my lips. My mouth felt dry. I wanted to get back to the sideshow tent.

"Would you care for some iced tea?"

I shook my head. "No. I was, *um*, going to watch the show. My dad said you needed this." I put the white bag on the table.

"Yes, unfortunately. Thank you, Angel. It's for my wife."

"Your wife?" I quickly closed my mouth, hoping my face didn't betray the surprise I felt.

"Yes. Melinda. She's in the show with me."

"The . . ." I almost said fat lady. "The lady who's supposed to be your mother?"

"Yes." He smiled. "You've seen the show before, then. Melinda's lying down right now. Hopefully she'll be up to our usual romp, although I'll go easier on her today." His smile faded away and he pushed himself off the cushion with a little jump. He crossed the squares of scuffed linoleum to the tiny fridge under the counter, took out a frosted pitcher, and pointed above him. "Glasses are up there. Are you sure you wouldn't like some?" His tone sounded casual, but underneath there was something else.

I licked my lips again. I didn't want to stay, didn't want to sit in this hot little trailer with Leon. I put my hand into my pocket, fingered the tickets, and opened my mouth to say no. Leon was clutching the icy pitcher and staring at me.

"Okay," I said.

"Just grab yourself a glass. Small and cramped as this place is, some things are still too high for me."

I opened the cabinet over the fridge and took out a plastic glass covered with neon pink dancing flamingos.

"Come. Sit." Leon climbed back onto his cushion. He filled my flamingo glass, then added more iced tea to his own. "The show won't start for at least twenty minutes. They always let people grow impatient. Gets 'em revved up and receptive."

I sat down on the bench and took a sip of my drink.

The tea was sweet, lemony, icy. I glanced toward the closed door at the end of the trailer.

"I'll wake her up in a few minutes," Leon said. "She's already in costume." He ran his fingers up and down his sweating glass. "The heat plays her out."

"It's hard on everyone."

Leon put the glass to his forehead and rolled it back and forth. "Melinda likes snow. The mountains. I met her at college, down in Colorado. That's where she's from."

"You went to university?" I smiled brightly as I said it, not wanting everything that came out of my mouth to sound surprised.

"Yeah. Got a degree in political science, but I couldn't get a job. Melinda was studying drama. She even did a few commercials. She's the one who got me into show business." His mouth twisted. "So to speak." He took a long drink, then set his glass down on the table. "This isn't exactly the career we had in mind when we started."

There was a heartbeat of silence. I tried to think of something to say.

"Don't you find it hard, traveling around all the time?" I asked, leaning back on the bench and resting against the wall.

"Sometimes. But it's a living, as the saying goes. We probably should have stopped a long time ago, when we were younger. Now there aren't that many options left open to us. Considering." He smiled again. He had a nice smile. "I know that look on your face. I see it all the time."

I ran my finger around the top of the glass, trying to make my face look blank. I shook my head.

"You want to know what it's like being this small, don't you? Everyone wants to know."

I looked at him. "I just wonder," I said, "if you feel bad being . . . different. Do you ever wish you were like everyone else? Do you ever wish you could just wake up and, well, fit in?"

"How old are you, Angel?"

"Fifteen next month."

He nodded, jiggling his glass so the ice cubes rattled. "I used to get really mad when I was younger. I'd wonder why it had to be me. Or I'd dream that somebody would discover some new drug and *presto*! I'd be the same size as everyone else. That's when I was just a kid. But there comes a time when you have to say, 'This is me. This is who I am.' And then you start thinking about what's really important in life." He ripped the white bag open and took out the small clear bottle, studying it. "And who's really important." He looked up at me. "Starting with yourself. Once you realize that you're important just as you are, you learn not to care so much about the people who stare, or who act like you're not there at all, or who use you because you're different."

I took another sip, then set my glass back on the table in the ring of water it had made. There was a sudden drumroll and a burst of applause.

"The show's starting," Leon said. "I better rouse

Melinda and get myself ready." He held out his hand. "Thanks for bringing this by, Angel. And thanks for the visit. I needed a lift today."

I reached across the table and shook his hand. "Thanks for the tea," I said.

It was almost dark by the time I'd made my way back to the sideshow tent. The fair looked the best at night, with all the lights from the rides turned on and the daytime dust and grime hidden from view. My dad was busy taking tickets from the last few stragglers.

Rick and the others were still standing near the Ferris wheel. Rod and Loreen were smoking, but they dropped their cigarettes when they saw me. Loreen ground hers into the hard mud with her toe.

I walked toward them and Rick stepped forward. "Hey, we figured you weren't coming back, Angel. The show's already started."

"Yeah, I know. Sorry."

"So, didya get us in?"

I looked back at my dad, who was tearing tickets in half for Mr. and Mrs. Van de Vorst. He looked up, saw me, and gave a little wave. I waved back, then put my hand in my pocket, closing my fingers around my own tickets.

I could smell Rick's spicy aftershave and could hear the *whoosh, whoosh, whoosh* of each Ferris wheel car as it passed over our heads. For just a second I felt a rush of dizziness, as if it were me going over the top in one of those shaky little boxes, my stomach lurching on the rush down.

I felt the smoothness of the tickets between my fingers and looked at Rick's lips. Then I thought about what Leon had said about knowing what's important.

I heard Mr. Van de Vorst's booming laugh, then my dad's quiet one. I looked back at him, and even from that distance I could see he had a smear of mustard on his chin.

I turned and started to walk toward him. I knew I'd better tell him about it. Mom would kill him if she discovered he'd been eating a Lean Mean one.

Love, Unrequited

Despite being of sound mind and body, and in the middle of my teen years, I have not known a great love – or even one of mediocre quality. Because of this lack, I have submerged myself in the love of others. I've rolled in it, soaked it up, swallowed it whole.

Although I have been attracted to a few of the boys in the small cliquish environment of my high school, their reaction to me is always less than overwhelming. Growing up in a farming community, and having prior intimate knowledge of each others' lives and the lives of every member of our families, has definitely dampened some of the enthusiasm for the typical boy-meets-girl scenarios. There is little we don't know about each other. Still, even with all this familiarity, romance did blossom between many of the students, but a year away from my final year of high school, I was still hoping for my first real love.

Because of my better-than-average grades all through school, the recent results of some provincial tests, and the urging of the school guidance counselor, my parents reluctantly agreed that I should go to university in the city when I completed grade twelve. I would be the first in our extended family of farmers to take such a leap. I welcomed the idea, was excited at the prospect of life in the city, and secretly hoped that somehow, somewhere in those stone buildings full of strangers, I would meet him – the nameless man I knew was out there waiting for me. But until that time, I had my books.

I've always read. I don't remember learning to read, or even coming to the exhilarating realization that I was actually reading. My mother said that one day, when I was about four, she walked into the kitchen and heard me reading the description of a humidifier from the Sears catalogue. After that I read anything available, from the Quotable Quotes in the stacks of musty *Reader's Digest*s under the basement stairs to the atrocious skin diseases listed in the *Everyman's Medical Journal* hidden in my parents' bedroom closet.

My family wasn't a reading family, dispelling the idea that voracious readers emerge from atmospheres of good role models and an abundance of available reading material. My father only read parts of the newspaper that he brought home from town on Saturdays, as well as instruction manuals for electric tools and small appliances. When he did read, it was out loud, whether anyone was listening or not. My mother just had her monthly issue of *Chatelaine* and the community bulletin that was passed out at church each Sunday.

Even when I was young, I knew it was hard for my parents to handle my obvious gift. But they did their best. Every Saturday evening, when we went into town, my mom would let me pick one of the Little Golden Books stocked in the rack at Hounslow's Dry Goods. My dad dropped me off at the small library over at High Point every month when he went to do his banking.

I remember my grade two teacher, Mrs. Ronquillo, making each of us color a xeroxed picture of a book with a smiling face on its cover. Under the picture it said BOOKS ARE OUR FRIENDS. That day after school, I made up a poem about books. I called it "My Secret Friend." I read it at the supper table, standing up and clearing my throat importantly before I started. But halfway through, as I paused for effect, my dad put down his spoon with a clatter. "I just don't like when you slice bananas into the jelly, Marilyn," he said. "They leave a real slimy taste."

"The kids like them," my mom answered. "Next time I'll use peaches. You like peaches, don't you?"

"I wasn't finished," I said.

"Weren't you, dear?" my mom asked. "Well, it was just lovely anyway. Now, are you going to finish your dessert, or can your brother have it? It's his favorite."

At that age I was still hopeful about my parents. "Did you like my poem, Dad?"

My dad nodded, working a browning banana slice out of his green jelly. "Real nice, honey," he said. "Hey now, I know a poem." He pronounced it *pome*.

He looked up, holding his spoon in the air. We all watched him. He started waving the spoon back and forth, like a magic wand, in time to his words:

"There was an old farmer from Carting,
Who never could stop his loud –"

My mother interrupted. "You just cut that out, Ray. You know I don't like the kids to hear that kind of thing." But she was smiling.

My dad winked at her. I folded my paper up, put it in the pocket of my jeans, and sat down again.

"I think your poem was stupid, Carla," my sister said. "How can you be friends with someone who's not even a person? That's stupid."

"Don't call your sister stupid," my mother scolded, piling the plates and glasses on the table. "Give me a hand with these dishes now, girls."

My sister pinched my arm, whispering, "Stupid."

But books really were my friends. And later, they became my solace in a world filled with disappointments. For a short girl with temperamental skin and hair the color of an aging mouse and a speech disorder, books grew to be more than mere companions. They were my world of love.

I first wept over the plight of animals facing lost love, usually the loss of mother love. Dumbo sneaking out to be rocked in his chained mother's trunk. Bambi and that terrible hunter business. Then I graduated to humans and their love for their animals, usually a boy and his dog, a girl and her horse. But before I was twelve, I had done away with animals altogether and wanted to read about love between people, how it shaped and tore apart and soothed, how it was really at the bottom of everything.

After reading innumerable books about the pain of human relationships, I realized that love, unrequited – love that is unreturned – was, for me, the saddest condition. It involved the slow strangulation of the aorta. The poisonous twisting of that great artery always lessened – cruelly, I thought – just enough to allow the victim to live, but in a state of constant deep pain and never-ending sorrow.

In the novels I read, there are many reasons for unrequited love. Commonly, the man was already married, or just in the process of falling in love with someone else. Perhaps, on the day the couple were to consummate their love, they were separated by a war, or one of them was sent on a mission of some sort and lost in action. In some cases, just after professing his love, a wonderful man might develop a grievous disease, often originating in the Tropics, which made him slowly go mad or take on a cold and unfamiliar personality. Or he could have been involved in a debilitating accident that caused the loss of his memory, and as a result he forgot his true love and fell for one of his nurses.

No matter what the reason, the outcome was always the same. The lives of heartbroken heroines filled my bookshelves, overflowing onto the floor. As I read through those pain-filled pages, I always knew how I would have reacted. I knew I could have helped avoid the problems that besieged the sad victims, women too proud, too overwhelmed by circumstance, or simply too weak to take control of their destinies. If I could have slipped between the pages of those novels, I could have averted much of the tragedy.

But as I dreamed of helping paper women, a similar melodrama, this one involving flesh and blood, began unfolding right in front of my eyes, in the chalky classrooms and dingy hallways of my high school.

It was a virulent case of unrequited love suffered by my English teacher, Madeleine Kleinfeld, for a man who had eyes for another.

I liked Miss Kleinfeld right from my first day in the grade eleven novel study class. I liked her old-fashioned, demure expression, the way she unconsciously placed her hand to her throat as she read a moving passage, her quiet steady voice and unflinching gaze. She often wore long flowing skirts and simple black sweaters that gave her pale skin a creamy glow; her fine, dark blonde hair was caught at the nape of her neck with a tortoiseshell barrette, and tiny gold hoops hung from her ears. She looked like someone who would be more comfortable reading meandering poems in a darkened room for a small but appreciative audience than standing, rather helplessly, in front of a large disinterested class of teenagers.

Most of the kids pretty well ignored her, slumping in their desks as she read parts of novels and tried to draw someone, anyone, into a discussion on the use of fore-shadowing or symbolism. The boys openly disregarded her, absently picking at calluses on their palms, or crack-ing their knuckles, or yawning huge noisy yawns that often ended in a burp – calling forth a sudden onslaught of answering burps. The girls feigned disgust at the male body noises, wrote and passed notes, or put on makeup. I longed to call out the answers Miss Kleinfeld wanted to hear, but I had learned many years ago, by grade three or four, that no one likes someone who knows all the answers. Besides, I could never trust my voice, so instead I studied the cover of the current novel under discussion, not daring to look up in case she saw the eagerness in my eyes and urged me to speak.

That had happened once, toward the end of September. Up until that time I had never attempted to say anything in class, although I had smiled often and nodded at Miss Kleinfeld's comments. Catching one such nod, she had gratefully pounced on me.

"Ah, Carla, I can see you know what I'm getting at. Even though Steinbeck wrote this particular novel over sixty years ago, he addresses an issue that is very much one of today's larger social problems."

I nodded again, my heart tripping a little, a horrible sense of déjà vu washing over me.

"Carla? Could you tell us the issue?"

I opened my mouth to answer, hoping for the best. I could be quite coherent in one-to-one confrontations, but these group situations usually didn't go very well.

"Th . . . th . . . the p . . . p . . . the pppppp . . ." *The plight of the homeless*, my brain screamed. That smooth cliché, just five words. I tried again. But the words, no matter how simple, wouldn't roll off my tongue. It was terrible, even worse than usual. Probably because it was the first time I had been called on to speak in this particular class. My stuttering ran a predictable course.

I couldn't go on, and simply closed my mouth and sat there staring at my fingers spread out on my desk. There were the usual snickers, and then a few seconds of strained silence. Miss Kleinfeld, realizing her mistake, said, her voice kind, "Perhaps you could stay after class a few minutes, Carla, and we can discuss your idea." Then she immediately went on to examine some other aspect of Steinbeck's writing, as if the whole miserable episode had never taken place.

I did stay after class that day, and from then on stopped in regularly to discuss certain novels or Miss Kleinfeld's comments about them. Alone with her, and somehow sensing she was an ally, I relaxed, and before long was able to speak to her with a minimum of the laborious effort that was needed when I was anxious or tired. She always

listened carefully, respectfully, as if she were really interested in what I had to say. She didn't finish my words or
sentences, or get that trapped desperate look I had often
seen on other teachers' faces when they waited for me to
finish speaking. We actually started having heated conversations about books we had read, and she lent me
some of her own that weren't in the school library. After
a few months I think I had started to love Miss Kleinfeld
just a little.

Because of these feelings, I couldn't stand to see her
heart being broken over Mr. Gauthier, the history teacher.

I could understand why Miss Kleinfeld had fallen for
him. He had a cool detached manner with most people,
but underneath I was sure there was a strength and a
certain . . . passion. He was a Rhett Butler, possibly even
a Heathcliff.

But by the time I realized how Miss Kleinfeld felt
about Mr. Gauthier, he was already hopelessly infatuated
with the new school secretary, Ms. Lola Pickell.

I manned the front desk in the office while Ms. Pickell
took her lunch break. The activities during lunch hour
consisted of team sports in the gym or walking. In bad
weather the walks took place up and down the hallways,
and when it wasn't too cold or too windy or raining or
snowing, along the road outside the school. The walks
were carried out in small one-gender packs, where the
real and imagined sex lives of other packs were examined

in great detail. Since I didn't excel at either sports or dis-
cussions on sex, I had volunteered for the office job.

I left the answering machine on, but listened in to the
messages in case there was a real emergency. For obvious
reasons I wasn't very good at telephone communica-
tions, but then there were never any earth-shattering
calls, just parents reminding their children to bring the
truck right home after school, or a textbook salesman
letting the principal know when he would be in with his
samples. I wrote down each message and personally
delivered them after lunch. I was also occasionally called
upon to dispense a bandage from the first-aid kit under
the counter.

Ms. Pickell always returned from her lunch at the
Midtown Café at exactly five minutes before one. It was
during one of these noon hours, just after Halloween,
that Mr. Gauthier came into the office as I was gathering
my books and tidying up Ms. Pickell's desk. She was
hanging her heavy sweater on a coatrack beside the principal's office. Mr. Gauthier walked behind the counter
and, putting his hand on the small of Ms. Pickell's back,
leaned toward her and said something into her ear.
Whatever he said made her laugh, a high small laugh. I
knew, just by his body language, that there was no way
he was discussing school politics. At that moment a
movement caught my eye, and I turned my head just
enough to see Miss Kleinfeld. She must have come in
right behind Mr. Gauthier and now she was standing at

the counter, a stricken look on her face. She put her hand to her throat in that familiar gesture, and her cheeks burned with two bright, fevered spots of color. Her eyes were riveted to Mr. Gauthier's hand, the hand that was applying gentle pressure on Ms. Pickell's back. In that instant I knew that Miss Kleinfeld harbored a secret love for Mr. Gauthier. The look on her face spoke as clearly as if she had uttered the words.

After that I saw the signs constantly. When Miss Kleinfeld came into the office to check her message slot just before the one o'clock bell, I saw her eyeing Ms. Pickell from under her pale lashes, all the while pretending to be engrossed in the files or absentee forms in front of her. Her face wore a haunted look as she studied Ms. Pickell's perfect posture and carefully groomed hair and small childlike features. I knew she was trying to figure out what Miss Pickell had that she didn't, what it was that so attracted Mr. Gauthier.

It wasn't difficult to understand. Lola Pickell was the kind of woman anyone would find attractive. When she first came to work at the school in the fall, the office had been full of nervously grinning boys for weeks. There was a run on needing to use the phone or the photocopier, all in the hope of standing close enough to Miss Pickell to smell her perfume or peer down the front of her blouse. Nobody knew where Ms. Pickell had come from. She kept her past a secret and didn't join any of the women's clubs, or attend any functions put on at the school or in either of the churches.

It was rumored that she was recovering from a lost love and had come to hide in our little community. I'm not sure how Ms. Pickell felt about Mr. Gauthier, but he certainly made his intentions clear. There were a number of arrangements of fresh flowers, all delivered to her desk from the only florist for thirty miles, way over in Fannystelle. I had to sign for them more than once, and I noticed the delivery charge was as much as the cost of the flowers. When I opened Ms. Pickell's top drawer to take out a pen, there was always a little box of Laura Secord fruit jellies or a tiny heart-shaped box of ginger chocolates. "To L. Love, M." was written on the top right-hand corner of every box. Maurice Gauthier was not original, but he was persistent.

I watched Miss Kleinfeld closely to see how she was taking the romance. I noticed how her narrow shoulders slumped as she tried to read the scribbled essays piled in front of her, how she suddenly raised her head and stared, unseeing, at the cracked wall at the back of the room. Instead of Madeleine Kleinfeld, I began to see other heroines, other women who had loved and lost.

Mattie Silver. Poor carefree Mattie, falling in love with the married Ethan in *Ethan Frome*. The hopelessness of their situation forced them into the disastrous suicidal sleigh ride, leaving Mattie, her spine shattered, forever prisoner in her worn armchair, much as Miss Kleinfeld sat imprisoned in her hard wooden seat.

As Miss Kleinfeld read a lengthy passage out of *Far from the Madding Crowd*, moving her lips over the familiar words, I saw Bathsheba's warm moist mouth begging her husband, "Kiss me too, Frank – kiss me!" as he kissed the frozen porcelain lips of his dead child-lover, Fanny Robin. My eyes blurred with tears more than once on those gray prairie afternoons, envisioning Miss Kleinfeld beseeching Mr. Gauthier to love her.

By March I was really worried about her. She was slipping deeper and deeper into the abyss of unrequited love. Her skin had taken on a papery quality and the shadows under her eyes were a violent bruised purple. Her clothes hung limply on her thin frame as she painfully rose from her chair and slowly wandered about the classroom and in the hallways. I wondered that no one else noticed, but then no one else ever paid much attention to Miss Kleinfeld.

She had lived in our town for five or six years. In that time, according to my Auntie May, who knew all the local gossip, Miss Kleinfeld had never dated any of the single men. Whether she had actually ever been approached was one of the only things my aunt didn't know. Auntie May operated the small postal station at one end of Munn's Drug Services, and had a lot of time on her hands. She loved being on the telling or receiving end of a juicy story. Madeleine Kleinfeld showed little promise in that department.

I found myself thinking about Miss Kleinfeld at odd hours. I seemed to be the only one to witness her angst, her tortured soul, her longing for Mr. Gauthier. And then one spring morning I woke up and realized that this was the opportunity I had been waiting for, had dreamed about. It was my chance to rescue Miss Kleinfeld from the grip of unrequited love.

As the year unfolded, I considered a variety of strategies. I could try to get them alone together, possibly by requesting academic help from both of them, getting them into the same classroom and then slipping out, leaving them facing each other in the empty room. Or, through my access to blank staff memo sheets in the office, I could conjure up a phantom meeting between the two of them. I clearly envisioned the scene. They would ponder the situation, and then, unable to understand what had happened, laugh merrily at the folly. Mr. Gauthier, hearing Miss Kleinfeld's tinkling laugh and seeing her girlish dimples, would wonder how he had missed her charm.

Another plan of attack, perhaps less childish and fault-riddled, involved the shallower side of romance. Miss Kleinfeld's personal style was that retiring kind of attractiveness that sometimes needs a little boost. I wondered how a makeover and new outfit could be tactfully suggested. With a new, more Lola-like exterior, Miss Kleinfeld would surely attract Mr. Gauthier's attention. Once he took an interest in her physical attributes, he would be open to discovering the gold mine inside.

I mulled over a dozen ways of getting Mr. Gauthier to notice Miss Kleinfeld. But before I could spring any plan into action, fate took over. And for once, it seemed that it was on my side. On the side of love.

Lola Pickell packed up and left town. On Friday, May 16, she was at her desk. On Monday the 19th, she was gone.

Of course, there were immediate whispered suspicions of the reason she left before the end of the school year. The boring possibility was that she had had a fight with the principal. One of the grade ten girls said she had heard loud voices from the office on the very Friday that was Ms. Pickell's last day. The other, more interesting possibility, and I believe this was started by my own Auntie May, was that an old lover had contacted Ms. Pickell with an offer she couldn't refuse.

To me, the reason Ms. Pickell left was unimportant. My heart sang at the possibilities. Mr. Gauthier must be aching, in need of consolation over the sudden departure of Lola, and Madeleine Kleinfeld could be a shoulder to cry on, a sympathetic ear. In no time she would move from comfort woman to love goddess. I hugged the secret knowledge close to myself at night, visualizing the slow awakening of passion, the ensuing heat of courtship, and the consequent joining of hearts and bodies.

Within a week I could see a hint of color returning to Miss Kleinfeld's cheeks. During class time, she now stood with a small pleased smile on her lips, staring out the window at the budding trees that lined the road in front of the school. She didn't seem to mind that assignments were late or sometimes not turned in at all, and she let us read whatever we wanted, as long as it was done quietly. She said we had covered enough for the year; we could relax for the last six weeks.

One afternoon, when I had finished my book and wanted to go to the library for something else, I went up to her desk. She was busily writing on a piece of lilac paper, and when I cleared my throat to get her attention, she jumped and covered the sheet with her arms, like a child protecting a test paper from a cheating neighbor. It could only have been a love letter.

It was on a Thursday evening, almost a month after Ms. Pickell had left, that I was witness to something puzzling. I went along with my mother when she drove into town to check on Auntie May, who had been in bed with a virus all week. My mother wanted to cheer her up with a small jar of last year's peach preserves and a few sprays of plum blossoms from the tree near our back door.

It started to drizzle as soon as we left the house, and by

the time we hit the edge of town it was raining with a steady quiet rhythm, the way it only does when summer is just waiting. Mom dropped me off at the Chinese restaurant with an empty quart sealer to pick up some wonton soup as well as half a dozen eggrolls to take home to my dad. When he heard we were going to town, he had made his usual joke about having a "yen" for some Chinese food. I had told him, more than once, that yen was the money used in Japan – in China they used yuan – but that didn't stop him. I gave my order to Mr. Chu, who impatiently tapped his long delicate fingers on the Formica countertop while he waited for me to finish. Then I sat on a red vinyl chair under the windowsill, idly looking at the deserted street through the leafy curtain of dusty geraniums in foil-wrapped pots.

As I sat there, watching a bony white dog sniffing along the curb outside the restaurant, I noticed a car backed into one of the diagonal parking spots across the street. There were two people in the car, and as I narrowed my eyes, focusing on their heads, I realized, with a shock of recognition, that it was Ms. Pickell and Miss Kleinfeld. Surprisingly, Miss Kleinfeld seemed to be doing all the talking. It was hard to make much out through the plants and the wet windshield, but I could see that Miss Kleinfeld's mouth kept moving, her hands rising and falling behind the dashboard. Ms. Pickell seemed to be studying her own hands on the steering wheel. She shook her head once, but I couldn't make out her expression.

Miss Kleinfeld reached over and laid her hand on Ms. Pickell's shoulder, and she nodded and turned to her . . . and at that very moment Earl McCutcheon's old half-ton pulled up outside the restaurant, completely blocking my view. I jumped up, trying to see around the truck, but all I could catch was the side mirror of the car across the street. Next Mr. Chu called me to tell me my order was ready, and as I finished paying, I saw my mom's car pull up outside. I hurried out with my soup and eggrolls, hoping to catch another glimpse of the pair across the street, but the car was gone, a large dry rectangle on the cement the only evidence that it had even been there.

I spent the evening in a state of mixed emotions. What was Ms. Pickell doing in town? Had the two women been arguing over Mr. Gauthier? I needed to know. I needed to find out what Miss Kleinfeld was feeling.

"Don't you think it's ironic, Miss Kleinfeld," I said slowly, after class the next day, "how, at the end, he just leaves her?" I looked down at the cover of the book I was holding. "I mean, I never imagined he would walk away after all they'd been through together. He should have loved her."

"Yes, it is ironic, Carla. But love doesn't always work out the way you expect it to."

I folded and unfolded the paper jacket of the book. "But I feel that it would be a stronger ending if he did fall in love with her. Don't you think so? Don't you think it's great when it all works out in the end?"

"Well, in that book I think the ending is realistic. That's why conclusions that are too pat are called story-book endings."

"But I like endings where everyone is happy."

Miss Kleinfeld briefly put her hand over mine. When I looked up at her, I saw that her face was somehow twisted. The smile was still there, but it was totally empty, a fixing of muscles. "Don't spend these precious years of your life worrying about the complicated whys of love," she said. "And remember, you don't always find happiness, or love, where you expect to."

She took her hand off mine and started stacking an already neat pile of test papers.

A few nights later, my mother brought a pile of clean clothes into my room. As she set them on the bed, where I was reading, she looked around and shook her head.

"Honestly, Carla, this is terrible."

"What?"

"Your room. It's a mess. When you shared it with your sister, it was always neat. Since she's moved out, I can see who really kept it clean."

"What's the difference? Nobody ever sees it." It was too old an argument to waste time on. I turned the page, not looking up.

"And it's almost dark in here. You'll ruin your eyes." She flicked on the light switch and the sickly glare from the overhead light filled the room. "And look, isn't that a library book? From school?" She nudged a book on the floor with the toe of her slipper.

"I guess," I said, looking down at it.

"Well, get it back before the holidays start. Remember what happened last year with all your overdue books? You don't want your dad getting in a state again. This time he just might not pay."

I pushed myself off the bed and sat down on the floor, my back against the bookshelf. My mother tsked to herself and moved things around on the top of my desk. As I sorted through a pile of books on the floor, I found a copy of *Madame Bovary*. I remembered borrowing it from Miss Kleinfeld ages ago, just after Christmas. "It's quite special to me," she had said, handing it across her desk. "It was the first hardcover book I bought. It was back in high school; I saved my baby-sitting money for a long time."

Now I had a rush of guilt, turning the book over in my hands. I wondered if she realized I still had it.

"And here's a notebook that belongs to Lisa Albright," my mother said. "Her name's right here. Why have you got her notebook?"

I ran my palm over the cover of the book, imagining Miss Kleinfeld buying it when she was about my age. I opened the cover. On the top right-hand corner of the first page was a large M, written in Miss Kleinfeld's spidery scrawl. As I stared at the M, it wavered and blurred for a second. I had seen her initials, M. K., dozens of times beside her comments on my assignments, under the marks on the top of my tests, in the front of other books she had lent me. I never really looked at those letters with any particular concern; they were almost as familiar as my own. But tonight that M stood out, seemed to bore into my brain. I had seen it somewhere else, somewhere I hadn't expected to see it.

To L. Love, M.

The room suddenly seemed too still, and in an instant grew so bright that I couldn't see anything. I was aware of an odd rushing noise starting at the back of my head, but working toward my ears. My mother's voice came from far away.

"Carla, you'd better take this to Lisa tomorrow. She might need it. Carla? What's wrong?"

I blinked a few times, the brightness fading. I saw the book slide out of my hands and drop onto the floor. My mother's feet, wide and flat in her old slippers with the fuzzy blue fur worn away everywhere but the very top, came into view.

"Carla?"

My mouth started its hateful working. "I th . . . think I'll go to b . . . to b . . . to bed now, Mom," I said, not looking up.

"Well, all right, but on Saturday you get busy on this mess," she said. I watched the slippers move away. "I don't know how you'll ever manage your own home if you –" The words were cut off by the closing of the door.

I got up and turned out the light. I didn't even bother to get undressed, just climbed back onto my unmade bed and pulled the quilt over me.

I lay there, hearing my father's faint hollering for my brother somewhere down by the barn and watching the darkness fill the square of the window. I kept arranging and rearranging the pieces that were suddenly falling, almost faster than I could keep track of them, into the puzzle. The pieces that were about Miss Kleinfeld, and about Ms. Pickell. The pieces that were about me.

And, of course, about love. Unrequited.

Looking Out for Dayna

Dayna first came into the Chicken Shack right at closing time one Friday night. When I heard the tinkle of the bell at the front door, I slammed down my screwdriver, thinking how inconsiderate some people are, coming in one minute before it's time to lock the doors.

It had been forty-five minutes since we last had a customer, so it was a good time to work on the vat three fryer. It was coming apart where the handle connects to the basket, and I was in the process of tightening all the screws when I heard the bell.

Martin, the manager of the evening shift, was at the back of the building, loading garbage into the dumpster and scraping the ice off his car windows. The other girls had all complained about the fryer, too, but it was obvious no one was going to do anything about it until it actually fell apart. Then Martin would probably just drive over to head office and pick up a new one. I can't tell you how that bugs me; most things are so easy to fix if you catch them right away.

I'd had this job since last year, and while I didn't love working with slippery chicken parts and frozen french fries, it wasn't too bad as far as part-time jobs go. For one thing, I could pretty well choose my hours each week. There were four part-time girls sharing the evening and weekend shifts, and as long as we all arranged with each other when we'd work, Martin didn't care. I'd even had a raise a few months ago, and it felt good to be making more than minimum wage. My brother, Josh, and I had this deal with my mother about a car. If we saved up half the money for a secondhand one, she'd lend us the other half. Josh and I figured we could start looking in another six months.

I pushed through the swinging doors from the kitchen, wiping my hands on my apron. "Can I help . . ." I started, but there was no one at the counter. In a far corner of the brightly lit room someone was standing perfectly still, looking out the window at the swirls of snow blown up by the February wind. It could have been a boy or a girl, wearing snow-coated sneakers, tight jeans, and a black leather jacket. Thick reddish-brown shoulder-length hair was caught in the turned-up collar.

"Did you want something?" I called. "Actually, we're just closing. I already turned everything off, but there's a piece or two of chicken left over, and some coleslaw if you want it."

"I don't want anything. I just came in to get warm. I'll go in a second." It was a girl, and as she turned around, I saw her name – Dayna – inscribed in white stitching on the sleeve of the jacket. Under the name was a curled snake – it looked like a cobra – with a big thickened neck, raised to strike.

I could tell that the girl was about my age and height, but she was a lot thinner. She was wearing heavy black eye makeup that gave her a sort of sick look. Or maybe not sick, just unhealthy. Her face and lips were white, really pale. I knew she didn't go to my school. I'd never seen her before.

I reached behind me to tie my apron a little tighter. It was impossible to look even halfway normal in the baggy shapeless uniform issued by the Chicken Shack, but if you kept the apron tight around your hips it helped a little. "It's really cold out there. Supposed to snow some more later tonight."

The girl nodded, then shoved her hands down in her jacket pockets as she turned to face the window again. She was shivering.

I stood there watching her. I'd always wished I had the nerve to wear a jacket like that, but I knew I never would. It just wouldn't look good on me. You need a certain body, a kind of . . . I don't know . . . air, to pull off that look.

Looking at Dayna in that jacket, her shoulders back like no one could tell her what to wear and nothing could ever get to her, made me mad, maybe even jealous, for a minute. I straightened my own shoulders. But then I saw she was still shivering, and when she put one sneaker up on the backpack that was thrown on the floor beside her, I could see that her feet must have been soaking. "Hey, listen. I was just going to throw out that chicken anyway. Do you want it?"

The girl turned back to me. "What do I look like? Some panhandler? I got money. If I wanted something to eat, I'd buy it. Like I said, I'm just getting warm."

"Okay, okay, forget it." *Touchy.* She acted as though I committed some crime by trying to be nice. Just then, I heard Martin banging in the back door. "We're closing now, anyway."

I came from behind the counter and walked toward the door. The girl crossed the room, her wet sneakers squeaking on the tiled floor. We reached the door at the same time and both just stood there for a second, as if we were waiting for something. Then she pulled open the heavy door, the burst of cold wind making her squint. As she went through, into the night, she glanced over her shoulder. "Hey, about the chicken. Thanks anyway."

"No problem," I said as the door closed, surprised at her sudden change of tone. I leaned against the wooden door frame and clicked the deadbolt in place. The girl stood in front of the store, looking left, then right, then, with her head bent against the wind, she started left, down the deserted street.

A few minutes later, as Martin was driving me home, I looked for her, but it seemed she had disappeared.

It was about two weeks before I saw Dayna again. She came into the Chicken Shack on Saturday afternoon, between lunch and supper. The only other customer was an older man having a cup of coffee and reading a newspaper.

This time Dayna wasn't alone. She was with a little girl, maybe kindergarten age, who was holding her hand. The little girl was all bundled up in a snowsuit, with a scarf wrapped around her nose and mouth, but Dayna had on the same clothes as the night I'd first seen her. Just inside the door she bent down and unwrapped the scarf from the kid's face. "What do you want, Emily?" She glanced up at the menu board. "Do you want a leg? Legs are yummy. And fries?"

The little girl leaned against Dayna. "I don't know," she said, her voice raspy and edged with tears. "I'm tired. Can't we go home yet?"

Dayna's voice was soothing. "Not yet, Emmy. Pretty soon. You'll feel better after you eat something." She took the girl's hand and led her to one of the tables, helping her onto the chair. She pulled off the girl's mitts and undid the zipper of the snowsuit, then came up to the counter.

"Hi," I said.

Dayna looked at me. "Oh, hi," she said, but she didn't smile or anything.

I leaned over the counter and studied the little girl for a few seconds. "You baby-sitting?"

"Sort of. She's my sister. Half sister." Dayna glanced behind her. The girl was just staring at the top of the table, her hands limp in her lap and her legs sticking straight out in front of her like a china doll.

Dayna turned back. "I'll have one of those kid's packs," she said. "With the chicken leg and the fries and the cookie."

"You get a drink, too. It's included in the price."

"Coke."

"That's it?" I said, my finger on the TOTAL button. "Just one meal?"

Dayna dug in her pocket and took out a handful of change and a key ring with one key on it. She dumped it all on the counter and looked at it, then peered up at the menu board again. I saw that the dark makeup around her eyes didn't cover the fact that she hadn't had a good night's sleep in a long time. "Give me another Coke," she said, picking up the key ring.

"Five sixty, altogether. That's neat," I said, pointing at the key ring and pushing the extra dime and three pennies back across the counter. The key ring was a clear acrylic heart. It was filled with liquid and had lots of little red and pink hearts floating around in it. Dayna just shrugged and stuffed it back in her pocket with the coins.

I got the meal and drinks ready, then brought them over to the table. "Here you go," I said, putting the basket of food down in front of the little girl. "There's a little puzzle in there, too. Maybe your sister can help you do it."

They didn't look anything alike – the little girl had dark blonde hair and different features – but there was something about the expression on their faces that was the same.

"Careful. The fries are really hot," I said, as Emily grabbed the ketchup bottle and held it upside down over her basket. "Cute," I said to Dayna.

"Yeah," Dayna said, reaching over to take the bottle and give it a few hard shakes. "She's okay. And she's pretty tough. You're tough, aren't you, Emily?" She pulled one of the girl's soft curls.

Emily nodded, carefully licking the ketchup off the end of a long french fry. "Yeah, Dayna. We're tough. We stick together," she chanted, almost like a memorized verse.

Dayna dropped into the Chicken Shack a few more times when I was working. She never ordered anything to eat, just a Coke, and then she'd sit at one of the tables for a long time, watching the traffic go by outside. I couldn't figure out exactly why she wanted to spend any time in a place like the Chicken Shack, with its greasy smell and scratched tables and bright fluorescent lights, but after a while I decided that it was simply a place to sit, somewhere to be. A lot of places won't let you stay unless you order food, but Martin was good that way. He never said anything about how long anyone stayed, as long as they were quiet.

I started to wonder about Dayna, wonder why someone who looked like her, so bold and unafraid, was always
alone and needed a place to go.

One night in early spring, when I had finished my shift
and Dayna was still there, I called out to her. "Hey,
we're closing now." I shrugged my arms into my jacket,
pulled the elastic off my ponytail, and combed through
my hair with my fingers. "Do you need a ride somewhere? My brother's coming to pick me up. We could
drop you off."

Dayna got up, hoisting the backpack over one shoulder. "No thanks, Lori."

For a minute I wondered how she knew my name, then
I realized that, like her name written on the sleeve of her
jacket, mine was sewn on the shirt pocket of my uniform.

"You sure? It's raining."

Dayna walked to the window and looked out, as if
she hadn't noticed. "Oh, yeah. Well, the rain's better than
the cold." She put her tongue out to touch a tiny sore
at the side of her mouth.

"My brother should be here in a few minutes," I said,
coming to stand beside her. There was silence. I got that
uncomfortable feeling, the feeling I always get when
nobody says anything. "So. How's your sister? What's her
name? Annie?"

"Emmy. Emily."

"She was really sweet. I know it's probably a drag most

of the time, having a kid around, but I always thought it would be fun to have a little sister. Josh, that's my brother, he's pretty useless."

As soon as my voice stopped, the silence jumped loudly in. "Actually, I've got a half brother, too." I didn't seem able to stop myself; my mom and Josh are always telling me it's something I better learn. "A really little one. Nathan. He's ten months. I've only seen pictures of him. He lives out on Vancouver Island, in Nanaimo, with my dad."

I couldn't believe I was telling Dayna about Nathan. I'd never even told any of my friends. It seemed sort of creepy, my dad with this new wife who was only ten years older than me, and now a baby.

Dayna still didn't say anything.

"Both my parents seem to screw things up. My mom's got this boyfriend, William," I said. "Not Bill, or Will. William. It has to be William." I said it slow, the word stretched out. I waited for Dayna to smile, but she didn't. She didn't even look at me, just kept watching the rain.

"William Weeny," I said. That got her to face me. "That's what Josh and I call him. His last name is Weinholtz, but we figure Weeny suits him better."

Dayna's nostrils flared a bit. "Does he live with you?"

"Are you kidding? You don't know my mother. She'd never let a guy live with her without it being legal. That's what she says. Legal." The rain was coming down harder now.

Dayna shifted her pack to the other shoulder. "Vaseline."

"Huh?"

"Vaseline. That's what I call my mother's boyfriend."

I didn't say anything, for once. I didn't want to break the spell of Dayna actually telling me something.

"His name's Vlassie. Darren Vlassie. But I call him Vaseline, right to his face. Talk about a slimeball."

I wanted her to say more, but just then my mom's silver Honda pulled up at the front of the Chicken Shack. "Sure you don't want a ride?"

Dayna glanced out at the car, then shrugged. "Okay."

"Bye, Martin," I yelled to the kitchen, then Dayna and I hurried through the rain to the Honda.

After Dayna was in the back and I jumped in the front, I looked over at Josh. "Josh, this is Dayna."

Josh turned around and gave his usual grimace – the one that was supposed to be a smile. "Hi, Dayna."

There was a quiet hi from behind me.

"So where do you live?" I asked, over my shoulder.

Dayna didn't say anything for a second. "Which way are you going?"

"Our house is on Morrow, you know, near the park."

"You can just drop me off at the lights on Worthington."

"Okay. You must go to Wyatt High if you live on Worthington," I said. Wyatt was the only other high school in the area besides my own.

"Sometimes," Dayna answered.

"Oh." I turned around and looked at the windshield wipers. "So did it start okay this time?" I asked Josh.

"Yeah," Josh grunted.

"I told you the battery cables needed cleaning." I turned my head sideways again, so Dayna could hear me better. "It was having trouble starting. I knew it was the battery."

"Lori always thinks she knows how to patch everything; always thinks she knows what's wrong," Josh said, his voice getting a little louder. I could see his eyes looking in the rearview mirror. "She can't leave anything alone." He glanced back to me. I punched him on the arm and none of us said anything after that.

When we dropped Dayna off at the lights, I turned around and watched her through the rear window. She wasn't going down Worthington. Instead, she was walking back along the way we'd come, the rain bouncing down around her.

I realized that I was watching for Dayna at work. I don't know why I thought about her so much, but there was just something that made me want to know more. Maybe because she seemed so different than the girls I hung out with.

I liked talking and found it easy to strike up conversations with most of the customers who came into the Chicken Shack. But when I tried to talk to Dayna, all that came out of my mouth was unimportant chatter. I was trying to fill the silences, trying to get her to tell me more about herself. But none of our conversations, if you could call them that, seemed to go anywhere, and I think that's the way Dayna wanted it. She only told me little pieces of things, beginnings of sentences, beginnings of stories. There didn't seem to be a lot of endings.

When April came, with its soft warm breezy evenings, Dayna stopped showing up. I asked Martin and the other girls, but no one had seen her. Since she didn't need to get in out of the weather, I decided she'd probably found another place to spend her empty hours, a place where nobody asked her prying questions and told her boring details about their own boring lives. But even though she wasn't around, I couldn't stop thinking about her.

One day, in late June, I looked up the name Vlassie in the phone book. There were only two, one on the other side of the city and one in our area, on Preston. I tried phoning a few days in a row, but each time I got an answering machine, with a woman's voice, businesslike, saying to leave a message if you were calling for Darren or Joan. I didn't really feel like leaving a message, so on a Saturday morning I took Obie, our dog, tied his leash to my handlebars, and rode my bike over to Preston Avenue.

When I found number sixteen, I rang the bell, unzipping my jacket. The morning had started out cool and windy, strange for June, but now it was warming up and

I was hot from the ride. I rang again, but no one came to the door. I could hear a little kid crying, faintly, but it might have been coming from one of the nearby houses or yards. As I turned to walk down the steps, I heard the door open. I whirled around, for one instant thinking it would be Dayna standing there in her tight jeans and leather jacket, but it wasn't. It was a man.

"Yeah?" he said. He was pretty good-looking, his blond hair long and brushed straight back. He had on jeans, a neatly pressed denim shirt, and a thin tie. Silk. He reminded me of someone on a soap opera, someone who could be either the hero or the villain, depending on the script.

"I was looking for Dayna."

"You a friend of hers?" He crossed his arms over his chest and leaned against the door frame.

"Yeah. I haven't seen her for a while and I was just . . . wondering about her."

The man kept looking at me, as if he hadn't understood what I said. He made me uncomfortable, but I didn't know why. I couldn't believe *this* was Darren. Dayna had given me the impression that he was some real slob, the undershirt and beer-belly type. This guy was nothing like that. He looked almost perfect, except for his mouth. His lips were too full, too rosy. And the bottom one stuck out, like a spoiled brat who's used to getting whatever he wants.

"Are you Darren?" I asked, rubbing my palms back and forth over my handle grips.

He smiled. "She's been talking about me. Well, Dayna doesn't live here anymore, and hasn't for a while. Not since, let's see, must be sometime in May. Not that she ever called this place home. She was always in and out – one day here, the next day gone. Even Family Services couldn't handle her. But I'm sure she's fine. Dayna knows how to look after herself." His voice was convincing.

"So you don't know where she is?"

The smile didn't fade. "If you're a friend of Dayna's, you know what she's like." I saw his eyes travel down my body and come to rest on Obie, who was sitting obediently by my left foot, his tongue hanging out after the run. "Dayna never brought anyone home. She was always secretive about her friends. Secretive about everything." He stared into my eyes. I wanted to look away, but couldn't.

Darren stepped farther out. "And she was a liar, too. You know that, don't you? Dayna lied about everything. You could never believe anything she said." He took another step forward. "Do you know what I'm saying?"

"She never said much to me. I didn't know her that well." I said it fast, feeling threatened, as if I had to protect Dayna and myself, but I wasn't sure why.

Darren smiled even wider, letting me know I'd said the right thing. "Better for you. You couldn't believe anything she said," he repeated. "She always made things up . . . for attention." He looked over my face, then his eyes dropped again and slowly traveled down the length of my body.

I turned away, giving a short jerk on Obie's leash. My face and neck and chest were hot and sticky, not just from the sun and the bike ride, but because it felt as if he'd looked right through my T-shirt and my jeans. It made me feel ashamed. I pulled the front of my jacket together and did the zipper all the way up. I realized my hands were shaking.

I jumped on my bike and pedaled away without looking back, Obie's toenails clicking on the smooth cement as he ran to keep up. I didn't stop until I was a few blocks from my house, where I undid my jacket and wrapped it around my handlebars. I rode the rest of the way home slowly, the wind fresh and clean against me.

Then, one beautiful day in August, I saw her again as I was walking Obie in the park. Everyone calls it the park, even though it's officially named Hester O'Halloran Park, after some heroic Canadian woman who died in World War II. It has lots of green space and groves of trees and a duck pond and a little bridge over a dry gully. Typical but pretty. There's also a playground area, and that's where I saw Dayna, sitting on a swing.

It was the first time I'd seen her without her jacket. Inside the Chicken Shack she had never taken it off, never even unzipped it. Today she had the sleeves tied around her waist. I hadn't realized how skinny she was. Her collarbone stuck out over the neck of her Guns N' Roses T-shirt and her eyes looked sunken. She'd also dyed her hair black, so her skin seemed even paler.

"Hey, Dayna," I said, pulling Obie to a stop, then jerking up on the leash so he'd sit. "What's up?"

Dayna leaned forward on the swing to smooth Obie's broad forehead. "Nice dog," she said. "A lab?"

I nodded.

"What's his name?"

"Obie. Short for obsidian. It's a stone. Shiny and black." I left it at that. I think I'd learned just a little about Dayna. I realized that I had to take it real easy and not scare her away.

Dayna kept rubbing Obie's head. "I like dogs."

"Do you have one?"

"No. I did once, when I was little and I lived on a farm."

"You grew up on a farm?"

"No. I just lived on one once." She raised her head. "I've lived lots of places."

I waited. Another beginning, but she didn't say anything more. "I guess it's exciting in a way," I said. "Moving a lot, meeting different people."

"Yeah. Sure. Really exciting." Her voice had no emotion. I couldn't tell if she was being sarcastic or not. For a minute I thought she was going to say something more, but suddenly Obie lurched ahead as a big gray squirrel leapt between two trees behind the swings. He pulled at the leash, panting and whining.

"Wanna walk with me? I can't hold this guy when he wants to go. This is his big treat of the day, his walk, and he gets really put out if I don't keep moving."

Dayna slid off the swing, picking up her backpack with one swoop. "Might as well," she said, tightening the sleeves of her jacket.

Obie pulled harder and harder, making us both jog along behind him. At first I could hear Dayna breathing hard just behind me, but after a few minutes I couldn't hear her anymore. I yanked with all my might on Obie's leash and looked back. Dayna was bending over, untying one of her sneakers.

I walked back to her. "What's wrong?"

"Just a blister." She was panting. "You might as well go. I've got somewhere else to be anyway. People to see." She pulled her sneaker off and slid her sock slowly down. The sock had a big dark patch of dried blood on it where it was sticking to her heel. I craned my neck to see the blister. It had turned into a big oozing sore.

"That looks awful," I said. I dug into the pouch around my waist. "I've got some bandages in here somewhere." I pulled two out. "Here, take these."

"You carry bandages?" The way she said it made me feel stupid, so I bent my head, fussing with the zipper of the pouch. When I looked up, she was staring at the sore on her heel.

"Come on. Take them."

Dayna pulled her eyes away from her foot, reached out, and took the bandages. I watched her put them on her heel, then pull her sock back up and retie her sneaker. She stood up, scratching the top of one arm, then the other.

"Well, like I said, I gotta go." But she looked down at Obie, who was sitting at her feet. She put her hand out and he sniffed it, then jumped up, resting his front paws on her stomach and giving one short cheerful bark. His tail swung back and forth. Dayna started stroking his head again, then looked at my hand, which was holding the leash. "Could I take him for a minute? For a run?"

"Sure, but he really goes. Hang on, or he'll yank the leash out of your hand." I handed over the leather strap and Dayna threw her backpack to me. It landed on the ground. When I picked it up, I was surprised at how heavy it was.

I heard Dayna say, "Come on, boy," and then they were gone, Dayna racing behind Obie, her jacket and her hair flying as he bounded across the grassy field between the path and the duck pond.

I trotted after them and finally caught up at the end of the pond, where Obie was snuffling at some soaked bread crusts. Dayna's flat chest was heaving. She had two bright spots of color in her cheeks.

"That was great," she said. "What a great dog." Untying the arms of her jacket, she let it fall to the ground.

She reached up and scratched at her neck, hard scratches that left red trails on her white skin. Next she scratched at her shoulder, under the sleeve of her T-shirt. It was almost as if she didn't know she was doing it.

"Look, Dayna," I said, unzipping my pouch again and taking out a pen, "why don't I give you my phone number?"

Dayna stopped scratching. "Why?"

"Well, you could call me."

Dayna stared at me, a tiny twitch starting in her cheek.

"I don't have any paper. Do you?" I looked at her backpack.

"No."

I picked up her hand and turned it over. It was really cold, even though she was still panting. I quickly wrote my number on her palm.

"There. You can copy it down when you get home."

Dayna stooped down and picked up her jacket. "Yeah. Well, I'll see you." As she started to tie the arms of the jacket around her waist again, there was a tiny *clink* and something fell to the gravelly path. It was the key ring with the heart. But there was no key on the ring now.

Dayna looked at it, then held it out to me. "You want this thing?"

I was so surprised I just stood there.

Dayna jiggled her hand, the heart making a tiny pinging against the metal of the ring. "You like it, so take it. It's yours."

I reached out and took it. The ring was slightly bent open, so any keys you put on it would probably slip off.

Dayna grabbed her backpack and, without saying anything more, turned and started walking away, not on the path but across the grass, toward a group of huge old pine trees. Beyond the trees lay the street, the one that eventually led to the south overpass. If it was really quiet in the park, with no wind and no kids yelling, you could hear the far-off roar of semis whooshing by on that overpass, heading out of the city to the Trans-Canada Highway.

I looked down at the key ring. It wasn't that great, just a plastic heart with a bent ring. I knew it would never work right, even if I took a pair of pliers and twisted the metal ring so it closed again. But I held on to it, my fingers wrapped around the warm plastic, and I watched Dayna until she disappeared into the thick black-green shadows of the trees.

Baba Lu

The life I had always known was lost forever when my baba had to have her toe cut off.

The toe, the second one on her left foot, had plagued her for years, crowding and pushing into the third one, and eventually moving right on top of it. It pressed painfully when she walked and she could only wear a big soft slipper with the rounded end cut out. She wore slippers everywhere, even when she went visiting or to church suppers at the Blessed Virgin Mary on Boyd Avenue. In winter she put a pair of Dido's old galoshes over them.

Finally the doctor decided the only solution would be to amputate, and because Baba would have to be in the hospital for a week after the surgery, Grandmother McLaren had to come and stay with me. Neither Mom nor Dad could take any time off work, and even though I begged and cried – protesting that I was old enough to be left alone for an hour each morning, over lunch, and

for a few hours after school; that most of my friends had
been baby-sitting for years; that it was insulting not to be
trusted, not to be considered responsible enough to look
after myself – my mother wouldn't hear of it. And so, on
a blustery March day in 1959, Grandmother McLaren
came to our house on Anderson in the north end.

I have no earliest memory of Grandmother McLaren, but
I do of Baba Lu. She was throwing herself on top of my
dido's casket. I was only three or four, but I understood
perfectly why she did it. Dido was inside that box and he
was going away forever. At that age I had often thrown
myself at my mother, hurtling against her legs as she got
ready for work, holding on to the thick nubby material of
her coat as if I could stop her from leaving me by grabbing her one more time. In the same way, Baba Lu was
trying to make Dido stay.

My mother denies the incident. "That was over ten
years ago, Natalie," she said, when I tried to ask her about
it. "You were so little, you can't remember things clearly.
I don't know what I was thinking, anyway, letting you go
to a funeral at that age."

Grandmother McLaren, on the other hand, just sort
of edged into my life, the way you one day notice your
teeth are crooked, but you never saw them growing that
way. My mother and I visited her exactly once every
twenty-eight days, the fourth Saturday of each month,

when we would take the bus to her still, dustless house in Charleswood.

On our monthly visits, Grandmother McLaren and my mother would talk while I looked at the books in her bookshelf. I was never allowed to take them out of the shelves because they were in some sort of order that I couldn't figure out. After Mom and Grandmother had talked awhile, mainly about boring things like someone's new job or baby, we had lunch. Lunch at Grandmother McLaren's was usually a clear soup she called consommé, floury potato scones, and a plate of jiggling headcheese. Grandma and Mom drank Earl Grey tea, and I got a glass of lumpy buttermilk that made my teeth feel as though they were coated with that scum that floats on hot milk. Dessert was either a yellowish custard or thin dry cookies. No matter how carefully I tried to eat the cookies, they always crumbled down the front of my clothes.

The only good thing about those once-a-month visits was that Baba Lu would have spent the day making *verenyky* and filling them with her plum preserves. When she served them, the *verenyky* dripped with melted butter and sugar. Baba knew I was always famished after lunch in Charleswood.

Grandmother McLaren wouldn't come to our house, except once a year, for supper on Christmas. I never asked why she didn't come any other time, but somehow I knew it was because she didn't like Baba. And she didn't like Baba because Baba wasn't born here in Canada. Baba was "one of those people," Grandmother McLaren once told my mother.

For the last few years I'd hoped something would change when the two grandmothers saw each other. But it never did. For a while I blamed Baba Lu because she wasn't the same when Grandmother McLaren came over. I was sure that if she just acted her regular way, laughing and making little jokes, hugging me, urging everyone to eat, Grandmother McLaren would see how nice she was and would like her.

But Baba Lu wouldn't do or say much when Grandmother McLaren came. She'd spend most of the time in the kitchen getting the dinner ready, and would eat without talking, unless someone asked her something. Then, as soon as we were all done eating, she'd start cleaning up the gateleg table she and Mom had pulled away from the living-room wall and had set up with the good dishes. Mom always said to leave the dishes, we could do them later, but Baba Lu wouldn't answer, and I'd dry while she washed. Grandmother and Mom would have another cup of tea in the living room; Dad listened to the radio.

Baba Lu didn't even look quite the same during those Christmas suppers. She wouldn't wear her apron, and she'd take out the one tube of lipstick she had, a dull red, and put a dry smear of it across her lips. It made her mouth look like someone else's, thin and hard.

When the dishes were all done, we'd exchange Christmas presents with Grandmother McLaren. Grandmother and Baba always had a gift for each other, but they never varied, except in color. Grandmother would give Baba a small glass bottle of bath beads – some years pink and mauve, some years different shades of blue or green – saying, "Merry Christmas, Luba." But she said *Looba*, instead of sliding her tongue against her front teeth between the *l* and *u* so it sounded softer, like *Leuba*. The right way.

Baba would say, "Tank you, Missus," and then would give Grandmother a white hanky that she'd embroidered with tiny delicate flowers, or a fancy *M*.

As soon as my dad left to drive Grandmother McLaren home, we'd get out the cards or a new game or puzzle I'd got for Christmas. Then Baba would bring out the big box of chocolates she always got from Uncle Taras and the three of us – Baba, Mom, and I – would sit around the gateleg table and play, or work on the puzzle and eat chocolates. We never said anything about Grandmother McLaren once she was gone.

Our house on Anderson was tall and narrow. Like most of the other houses on our street, it had a glassed-in veranda on the front and the whole house was covered with pebbly gray sheets that were supposed to look like brick. Our window and door frames were painted a rusty brown that my mother called maroon. Inside there was a long skinny dark living room with a sunny kitchen behind. Two bedrooms and a bathroom were upstairs.

The house had a tiny backyard with a clothesline that stretched from a pole at the back step to another pole at the fence at the end of the yard. There was no front yard; the steps came down from the veranda almost to the sidewalk. In the narrow two-foot space between the pavement and the foundation of our house, a few scraggly but brave clumps of grass competed for room with bristling thistles and crumpled Oh Henry! and Sweet Marie wrappers. The garbage blew in from Adelman's Grocery next door. Adelman's was on the corner of Anderson and Salter, and I had to run in and out of the store at least four times a day for things Baba Lu needed for her cooking and baking.

Unless it was bitterly cold, there were always men sitting on the rough wooden bench outside Adelman's, smoking and talking. The uneven sidewalk in front was littered with an endless array of cigarette butts, more candy wrappers, and rosy glistening wads of well-chewed gum. Baba Lu got mad about the debris blowing up against our house, and every few weeks she'd shuffle out and yell at whoever happened to be passing the time of day on the bench at that moment, calling them lazy bums – except it always sounded like lazy bombs – and telling them to pick up their own garbage. The men would nod politely, and once Baba Lu retreated back into the house, would continue with their conversation.

Mr. and Mrs. Adelman never closed their store. They lived in the back and only locked the front door when they went to bed at night. Sometimes Mrs. Adelman would motion for me to come into the tiny crowded kitchen behind the linoleum-covered counter. She always wanted me to have a bite to eat. "So skinny, Natalie," she'd say, wringing her hands and pinching my cheeks. Then she'd offer me matzos spread thinly with sharp horseradish, or a spoonful of steaming chicken broth swimming with eyes of fat, or a nut-powdered cookie shaped like a slice of the moon.

Mrs. Adelman and my baba sounded alike when they talked to me. On one of the visits to Charleswood, one right after a Christmas, I heard Grandmother McLaren talking to my mother about the way Baba Lu spoke.

"She came here as a young woman, after all," Grandmother said, shaking her head, "and I still can't understand her, with that broken English of hers."

I didn't like the sound of that phrase, "broken English." Baba did have a language of her own when she talked to my mother and me, but it didn't sound broken. The words seemed to twist under and around her tongue in a pleasing rhythm, although it wasn't the magical melody of the words she whispered to me when she patted the covers over my shoulders at night, or smoothed my hair away from my forehead when I was sick. I always wanted her to teach me the secret language she kept for my father and her friends, but whenever I asked her she would just shake her head sadly, as if she would really like to but wasn't allowed.

Every day was the same, familiar and safe, with my baba waking me up for school by tickling my ear with a corner of the blanket, braiding my hair with fingers that felt like sparrows building a nest, and waving to me from the front step as I left. At lunch, between mouthfuls, we played cards – rummy 500, double solitaire, or cribbage. We ate thick purple borscht floating with islands of sour cream, or dark pumpernickel bread smeared first with hot mustard, then with chopped-up liver, boiled eggs, raw onion, and garlic – of course, garlic – all mashed together. Almost everything Baba made that wasn't sweet had onions and lots of garlic. The only time she didn't use them was in the Christmas meal. Mom said she could put an onion – one small one, chopped very fine – in the turkey stuffing, but no garlic. It was the only meal Mom ever talked to Baba Lu about.

After three-thirty I sat at the yellow Formica table with Baba and her friends from the neighborhood. They stopped by all the time during the week to talk, eat sunflower seeds, and drink black coffee or glasses of tea. One of the friends, I forget which, would hold a sugar cube between her back teeth and slurp loudly around it. They all had wonderful names, always ending, like Baba's, with the letter *a* – Marika, Orysia, Lesia, Daria. Every afternoon, as soon as I walked in the door, Baba Lu would call me to come and join them, and I was welcomed into their club, becoming a member when they called me Natalka instead of Natalie.

I listened to their funny stories about what Mrs. Rosenblatt had yelled at Mrs. Markewitch in front of Oretzkis's and who Mr. Kaminski's niece had been seen with at the College Theater. Cracking sunflower seeds loudly, I held tight to my pink sticky drink that smelled like summer.

Once every year, on a Sunday, Baba Lu made my dad drive us out to Winnipeg Beach to eat a picnic lunch. Then Dad would wait while Baba and I collected brown bagfuls of wild roses from the prickly bushes that grew up and down the dusty side roads.

Instead of sitting up front between Baba Lu and Dad for the ride home in the old panel truck, I would stretch out on a blanket spread on the floor in the back. Tired and hot in the gritty wind that blew in the open windows, my nose and shoulders tight and crackly from the sun, I would keep my face in one of the bags, inhaling the cool sweet scent of the petals. The next day, having mixed the petals with water and lemon and sugar and spices, Baba would boil up a big pot of thick syrup the color of the roses, and would pour it into old mayonnaise jars. I would help her carry the warm jars down to the wooden shelves that lined one wall of the basement, and we'd make room for them between the pickles and jams. Every week, all fall and winter and spring, she would

bring up a new jar and I would have my daily cordial of
summer, diluted with boiling or cool water depending
on the temperature outside.

The house, the street, and Baba Lu were all I knew. My
parents were little more than shadowy figures during the
week, going to work before I was up and coming home,
slumped and silent, often after Baba and I had finished
supper. My father hated having my mother work, but
we all knew that if she didn't, we couldn't pay the bills.
Mom said she didn't mind her job. She worked in the
lingerie department at Hudson's Bay, helping ladies try
on brassieres and corsets. She usually did an extra shift on
Thursday and Friday nights, sometimes even on Saturday
mornings. She had planned to be a secretary, and had
started a stenographer's course after high school. But
then she met my father at a skating rink one winter not
too long after the war – when he still had a thick pink
ribbon of scar tissue over his eyebrow – eloped with him
a few months later, and never completed her course.

Grandmother McLaren was horrified at my mother's
choice of men. On one of our Saturday visits, when I was
pretending to do homework but was really drawing elab-
orate triangles in my scribbler and eavesdropping, I heard
her talking about my mother's sisters. She droned on
about how their lives were easier because they had
married respectable decent men – one a manager for a

large company that sold tractors and farm equipment, the other a loan officer in a bank. These were good hard-working men, whose last names ended in a consonant, not a vowel.

I drew hard black lines through the triangles. My father *was* a respectable decent man, and he worked hard, too. He just couldn't find the right job – one that made him happy and paid him enough so Mom didn't have to work.

Finally he and Uncle Taras started their own business, a successful one that began to make real money right around the time of Baba Lu's operation and Grandmother McLaren's sojourn on Anderson Street.

The house was hollow and lifeless without Baba Lu. I didn't want to share the bedroom with Grandmother McLaren, so each night my mother made up a bed for me on the scratchy hard sofa in the living room. The darkened room with its tall ceiling was cold and whispery at night, and the huge flowers on the wallpaper turned into glaring unfriendly faces in the dimness.

Grandmother McLaren and I ate our breakfast and lunch in respectful silence, broken only by her polite questions about school and friends and my equally polite answers. I would kiss her rouged cheek before I left for school each morning, knowing it was expected, and would breathe in the delicate lavender scent of the eau de

toilette I had seen her place on the cutwork doily on
Baba's dresser. I missed Baba Lu's smell of onions and
garlic and Jergens.

On the night before Baba Lu was scheduled to come
home from the hospital, I lay on the sofa, my eyes tightly
closed, while I listened to Grandmother McLaren's mur-
muring in the kitchen.

"Honestly, Lenore, how can you live in a place like
this? And worse yet, bring Natalie up here! Doesn't that
husband of yours have the sense he was born with?"

"This area has always been his home, Mother. He likes
it. And Natalie –"

"Natalie! I'll tell you, Lenore, something dreadful
will happen to the girl if you don't get her away from
here, believe me. Haven't you noticed that she's growing
up? That she's," her voice sank on the next word,
"developing?"

The hushed tone of that simple word made me feel
suddenly shivery and ashamed. I thought I was causing
some kind of unspeakable trouble because my breasts no
longer lay flat and guiltless under my clothes.

"The things that happen around here!" Grandmother
McLaren carried on. "All those men lined up on that
bench next door, their sly eyes following every move. But
because you have to work day and night, you're not home
enough to know what goes on in your own neighborhood
– not that it ever was, or ever will be, *your* neighborhood,

Lenore. Some of the characters that pass right by your front door are enough to make my blood run cold. At the very least, if you do stay here, Natalie will fall in love with one of these Polacks, or another Hunkie, and then she'll end up like you, working herself to the bone, and for what? These people don't know about any of the niceties, they're just DPs, after all . . ."

"Mother! Stop it! You can't talk about my life that way!" My mother's voice had an unfamiliar edge. I had never heard her argue with Grandmother McLaren, and I almost sat up on the couch when I heard that note of anger in her voice. The unexplained shame about my father, Anderson Street, even my body, was replaced by a moment of hope; Mother would tell Grandmother McLaren to mind her own business and leave us alone.

But as I lay waiting, holding my breath, a harsh rasping sound started. It was the sound of my mother crying. I pulled the blanket up around my ears and, crossing my arms over my offending chest, closed my eyes again. For real this time. I knew there would be nothing more to hear.

Six months later we moved from Anderson Street to a new suburb on the edge of the city. My father tried to persuade Baba Lu to come with us; her foot hadn't healed properly and it was still difficult for her to get around. But she didn't want to come, arguing that all her friends were around her and she was too old to change. The house was sold, and Baba rented a main-floor bachelor suite in the apartment block on Cathedral, a few streets over from Anderson. Her friend Orysia lives on the second floor, and sometimes they eat supper together.

Our house is a new bungalow that has three bedrooms, a bathroom plus a powder room, and a paneled rec room in the basement. Outside the streets are wide and clean. Quiet.

Mom quit her job. Dad is teaching her to drive so she can go to university and take a course in English literature one evening a week.

Grandmother McLaren comes for dinner often now, usually on Sunday. We eat gray dry slabs of roast beef and Yorkshire pudding, covered with thick starchy gravy. Mom is still learning to cook. She phones Baba Lu for recipes, but all of Baba's recipes are in her head, so it's hard for her to tell Mom exactly what measurements she uses. When Mom tries to make the food we ate on Anderson Avenue, the *pyrohy* and *holubtsi* and *pyrizhky*, nothing ever tastes quite right. Mom thinks maybe Baba Lu forgets to tell her some of the ingredients.

Yesterday I watched Grandmother McLaren chew her food carefully, thoughtfully, sitting at our new lace-covered cherry table in the L-shaped living-dining room. I followed her gaze out to the pretty, lifeless street, and thought about what Baba Lu and I had talked about on the phone.

Starting next week, I'm going to take the bus to her apartment every Saturday. Baba Lu will have *verenyky* for me and she's going to show me how to cook something different each week. I'll make sure I write down the ingredients so I get them just right.

Saying Good-Bye

This is the first summer I've been to the Island without my dad. It's also the first summer I've been alive and he hasn't.

Sitting in my aunt and uncle's house, I watch Delia stuff a thick slice of warm homemade bread into her mouth, then chew slowly, her teeth showing, her eyes staring at the gently smiling face of Jesus on the wall in front of her.

The ancient calendar is thumbtacked to the wallpaper of golden teapots and pink and green daisies; the year at the bottom of the curling yellow page is so colorless it's hard to read. Nineteen seventy-something, three or eight. Over Jesus's halo the faded words "And Ye Shall Be Touched by Him" are followed by a smaller, even more faded message – "A Prayer from the Ladies of St. Winifred Chapter." The calendar has hung on the wall behind the table as long as I can remember – ever since I was a little kid and had first started coming to the Island with my dad. Even though everything else has changed, the calendar is still there.

With a noisy swallow, Delia reaches for the long bread knife and starts to carefully saw through the crumbling loaf.

"Cut a piece for Liza," Auntie Yvonne says, love shining from her glittering black eyes as she looks at Delia, her youngest child, the only one left at home now. Then her gaze moves reluctantly to me. "Liza could use another slice. We don't want your mother thinking we don't feed you, do we?"

I shake my head. Delia ignores her mother and, with the same knife, spreads a huge blob of butter over the soft surface of her bread, then, looking at me, licks the last creamy smears off the knife, her quick pointed tongue caressing the sharp edge. "Pass the jam," she says, her tongue around the blade.

"The strawberry, or the chokecherry?"

"Strawberry."

"Delia, didn't you hear me?" Auntie Yvonne says, wiping her wet hands on a tea towel and pushing back a strand of shiny black and dull gray hair that had come loose. The veins on the backs of her hands are raised and ropy as she starts to slice through the loaf with a clean knife.

"It's okay, Auntie. I'm not hungry." I smile to show that I don't mind Delia being rude.

My aunt looks at me, then suddenly her lips begin moving, trembling against each other the way rose petals do when a summer breeze blows up. Covering her mouth with her hand, she quickly turns back to the sink.

I know why she's crying. It still happens to my mom sometimes. Everyone's always said that my smile is exactly like my dad's. I try to remember, but sometimes I just forget and smile right at the people who loved him most.

The Island was his home. He grew up here, with his parents and his big sister, Yvonne, on this tiny tree-covered bump right in the middle of Lake Winnipeg. There are only fourteen houses scattered between strands of scrawny jack pine and whispering aspen and poplar, and just about everyone is related in some way.

Mostly older people live on the Island now; their kids usually go down to the city – or maybe to Riverton or Selkirk – to look for jobs. They can't make enough money fishing anymore. Besides Delia, there are just Billy Linklater's kids, a whole bunch of them. Ronette's the oldest, the same age as Delia and me. Delia can't wait to leave; she says in another year, as soon as she's sixteen, she's going to stay with her cousin Willa, who rents a house in Lockport and has a job at the Crazee Fun Water Slide in the summer and the Lockport Hotel in the winter.

The Island's real name is Loon Island, but no one calls it that anymore, not since my dad was a baby and all the kids started coming home from the school on the mainland saying that the white kids called them Loonies. My dad used to laugh about that story, saying no one would mind being called a Loony now that it means money. Back then it just meant crazy.

The Island feels different without my dad. When we came for our three weeks every summer, just the two of us, we'd stay in the little fishing shack right down by the water, curling up in sleeping bags on musty blown-up air mattresses. But we'd eat up at the house with Auntie Yvonne and Uncle Mort and whatever kids were around that year. Every night, before we went to sleep, Dad and I would lie on our backs in the long sweetgrass beside the shack and watch the sky, and he'd point out the constellations, and tell me the old Ojibwa legends, and what the Island was like when he was a boy, and stories about me as a baby.

My mom never came with us. She said she'd had a taste of Island living the summer she met my dad, and she'd rather relax in the city, thank you very much. She hadn't been back since the summer they'd met, when she came up as a university student on a youth grant to help record data for the fisheries ministry. My dad said she was like a snow angel, with her long white-blonde hair and pink skin, and he was so enchanted with her that he gave his boat and all his fishing gear to Delia's oldest brother, followed Mom back to the city, got a job in construction, and married her.

This summer was my mom's idea. I didn't want to come, but she said it would make me feel less lonely for

Dad, remembering all the good times with him when he was big and brown, with a laugh that echoed across the water at night – not the sad yellow stranger in a hospital gown that he was for most of my thirteenth year and part of my fourteenth.

And you have a job to do there, she'd said with a stern look, as if I could ever forget what my dad had asked me to do.

So far the whole week has been a total disaster. Without Dad there doesn't seem to be anything to do, and I feel like a stranger, a tall skinny girl with short blonde hair and narrow black eyes.

I don't have to stay any longer than I want; someone goes across the lake every day before ten. All I have to do is show up at the big dock with my backpack, get a lift to the mainland, walk the three blocks to the Bun's Up Bakery where the bus stops, and phone my mom to meet me at the bus station at 6:45. Each day I think that today's the day I'll do what I came to do, but then I lose my nerve.

Auntie Yvonne has tried hard to make me feel welcome, but Delia is another story; she's never liked me, even when we were both dumb little kids. She'd act all sweet and friendly when Dad was around, but as soon as he'd go off to visit all his old buddies she'd turn nasty, taking me to parts of the Island I didn't recognize and then running away and leaving me there, or telling me scary stories about vicious Island bears or the lady with a face like an old map who lived in a tiny log house down near the water.

Even though Delia can't scare me anymore, she still finds ways to make me feel stupid.

When she finishes her third piece of bread and jam, we go out to sit on the roof of the fishing shack, looking at the lake. After a while Ronette comes by and climbs up to join us. It's hot, so hot that even the flies seem to be buzzing slower than usual.

"Want to go swimming later?" Ronette asks. She's pretty nice – probably because she's the oldest and is used to sharing everything, including her mother's attention.

"Sure," I say.

"How about you, Delia?" Ronette asks, poking Delia's shoulder.

Delia jerks away from the jabbing finger. "Cut it out, Ronnie. I'll think about it." She pulls a folded *Teen Star* magazine out from the back pocket of her shorts. "Hey, did you see the latest picture of the Screaming Ravens?" She opens the magazine and hands it to Ronette.

"Cute," says Ronette, as she looks at the smudged sheet, then passes it to me. I glance down at the blurry photo of the band and give the magazine back to Delia.

"So, don't you think the lead guitarist is something?" she asks me.

"Yeah, he's okay," I say. I've never been into heavy metal.

Delia won't let it drop. "I can't believe you don't just *die* when you look at him. I mean, those lips! I bet he's a fabulous kisser. Don't you think he'd be a good kisser, Liza?"

I study a leaf stuck to the side of my bare foot. "I guess," I say casually. Hearing the smirk in Delia's voice, I look up.

"She *guesses* so, Ronette." She turns toward me again. "I *guess* you wouldn't know, would you, Liza? You've never kissed a guy, have you?"

I pick the leaf off, ordering my cheeks and neck not to turn that horrible dull red that shouts to everyone how I'm feeling. I inherited my dad's eyes and smile, but my mom's hair and skin. "If I haven't kissed anyone, Delia – and I'm not saying I haven't . . ." I said, pausing for effect and thinking about Danny Mitchell's embarrassing attempt in May after the block party, "it's because I haven't felt like it." I didn't add that even when I have felt like kissing someone – for example, Danny's best friend Bryan – they didn't always pick up on that feeling.

"Don't make me laugh," Delia shrieked, then proceeded to do so, throwing back her head and letting out a bray that sent a sparrow perched on the eave flapping straight up in alarm. "Princess Liza hasn't felt like kissing anyone. Pretty weird, eh, Ronette? Not to feel like kissing a boy? *Oh-oh,*" she kept on, moving away from me, her bottom scraping across the old shingles and sending particles of gravel rolling down the roof, "maybe she's the type that isn't interested in boys at all. *Oh-oh*," she repeated, giggling and fluttering her eyelashes at me.

Ronette stood up suddenly, her knees bent on the steep incline, and shielded her eyes with her arm as she looked out at the gray-green water. "Looks like Douglas is coming in. Let's go see if he brought the mail." She leapt off the low roof, landing in the grass with a muffled *thud*.

Delia got to her feet, supporting herself with one hand as she cautiously made her way to the edge. Then she jumped off heavily.

"Come on, Liza," Ronette called up. "Walk over with us."

I looked down into her round face and smiled gratefully. "No thanks, Ronette. You go on. I'm going to stay here for a while. If it doesn't cool off, I'll meet you at the dock later for a swim."

I don't go for a swim. Instead I take a long walk up to North Point, past the caved-in Anglican church with four broken pews still inside. I automatically start to hold my breath as I get close to the tiny graveyard a hundred meters from the church, then blow it out with an irritated noisy whistle. I'm too old to believe in that junk about breathing in the spirits of the dead that Delia told me when we were seven or eight.

I stop and look at the three rows of tilting wooden crosses inside the peeling white picket fence. No one's been buried here for at least twenty years, Auntie Yvonne told me, not since the big new church was built on the mainland and the minister stopped coming out. The mainland cemetery holds the Island people now.

As a soft cool draft blows up from the water, I think, for at least the hundredth time, about the container in my battered old green backpack, then I turn and walk back to the house.

Later, after supper, when all that's left of the sun is a thin streak of shell pink in the sky over the water, I ask Auntie Yvonne for a sleeping bag. She just nods, and when she hands it to me, she squeezes my shoulder so hard it hurts. She looks as if she wants to say something, but her mouth stays a straight sealed line. Delia looks up from the couch, where she's flipping through another magazine, and for once even she doesn't say anything, just puts her head down and starts flicking the pages faster.

I spread the sleeping bag beside the fishing shack and sit cross-legged on it. I wait, for maybe ten minutes or maybe an hour, until the sky has turned from black felt to a bold, gloriously sparkling blanket and the lake's night wind is blowing with quiet persistence. Then I pull the small metal canister out of my backpack. Its heaviness still surprises me. I unscrew the lid and look down.

Standing up, I tip the canister and watch the wind carry the ashes away. Then I lie down on the sleeping bag and stare up into the sky, waiting. The wind blows my hair against my cheek, and suddenly the summer smell of the water and the grass combine in an almost unbearable sweetness. I take a deep breath, and for the first time in a long long while, feel my eyes start to close in that easy perfect way that you know means you'll slide into sleep peacefully, without remembering what you don't want to remember and without worrying about things that make you so tired that sleep won't come.

I think about the ride home tomorrow, and about how I'll buy two boxes of Junior Mints for the trip, and about the feeling of my mom's arms around me as I step off the bus.

Acknowledgments

Special thanks to Jon and our children, Zalie, Brenna, and Kitt, for their constant encouragement and support. Also thanks to Kathy Lowinger, my editor, for her insight and her ability to help me see things in a clearer light. And a final thank-you to Melissa Kajpust and Deborah Froese, who give me hope with their wise words on writing, life, and all possible combinations of the two.